HARKLORD

The Bloodsh

Raphael White

ISBN: 9798778947764

Dedicated to Grandma Lily

CHAPTER ONE

A KING'S DEMISE

The elderly Duke watched with the tracking eyes of a feline as King Mortimer's worried wife paced back and forth in the throne room of Castle Wormwood.

"Our spies from the North will arrive in this castle within the minute. We shall learn whether or not King Mortimer succeeded, and if he lives to tell the tale himself."

"But Duke Gallance, I bear his child. If he should be dead, the responsibility this child shall have! And the likelihood is that the invasion shall begin as soon as winter properly ends - giving the child a sole month before they arrive, and thus meaning that he - or she - will be merely a baby when the battle begins! We will be without an inspiring leader."

Duke Gallance leaned back as he stood before the two thrones, one empty, one full, unfazed by the possibility that King Mortimer could be lying dead on enemy turf.

"We have plenty of leaders," he drawled, "I being one of them. Our barracks are full of poisoned arrows and sharpened swords. As well as our swords, our spears have also been specially readied, made with light mahogany poles for aerodynamic ability and a strong impact designed to shatter a Tyran's skull. Even if our King Mortimer were dead, we are prepared for a long siege. Those brutal Tyrans should know that we will be awaiting with burning oil and heavy, sharp rocks, ready for their attack. Oh, how the invaders shall suffer when they come." A thin smile spread to Duke Gallance's twisted and wrinkled lip, and his eyes seemed to gaze off into thin air.

A small man, perhaps of five feet, entered the room.
"Your majesty. Duke Gallance. Our spies have returned - do not be shocked at the blood on their clothes - they were attacked by bandits while on the road here. Their cart was pillaged and only two of the spies remain. They are waiting in the dinner hall below." The servant left. The silence continued, until it was rudely broken. Two guards either side of the door the servant had come

through almost silently whispered to each other. Despite their quietness the Duke heard.

"You fools," he hissed, "do not gossip about your King in the presence of her majesty the Queen of Rosewick." His sharp voice split through the air of the throne room as the Queen of Rosewick rose from her heavily embellished seat. The queen suspected she heard a spark of sarcasm in his voice.

"Shall we, Duke?" He raised his hand to bring her down from the raised area of the throne room. She stared at it briefly as if it were a dead rat, and walked down alone.

She still wondered why her husband liked Gallance. The Duke of Halcore was an unpleasant man at best, and almost always was at his worst: a bitter old man capable of violent mood swings from sarcastic to blatantly rude. He went insane when things were done improperly, and had been useless in combat since his leg was made permanently numb by a few free Goblins. He despised all Goblins, Gnomes, and everything that reminded him of his uselessness. Perhaps her husband found him good company; he had once been known to pull an odd joke or two when he was drunk and on the occasions he had emptied the wine cellar, they were actually humorous.

Or even perhaps Mortimer believed that the Duke was a link to his father, King James II. The two had been close friends while they warred against the neighbouring purple and orange banners of Starbill and had remained allies since. Halcore, of course, was one of the biggest towns in Rosewick and the duke of Halcore was often the king's staunchest ally and advisor. When it came down to it, the only reason why Mortimer kept Gallance around was because he had to. As Queen Arora thought this, she and Gallance began to regally make their way through the throne room and unto the castle.

*   *   *

The night was cold, but as many expected, the inn was warm. Wood burned in a fireplace, and a consistent stream of smoke exited the building via a heavy brick chimney. Inside, loud and inebriated chatter filled the large room, sending everyone there who was still sober into a spasm of madness, thus leading them to drink, and become drunk.

"Our king is likely dead in a ditch in Tyran lands," slurred one of the drinkers, "His wife's carryin' a baby an' she'll be sick soon. The best man we've bloody got's the bloody Duke of Halcore. An' he's a right ol' devil, 'e is." The man's breath stank of wine and he was insisting upon telling his story to the whole bar. A young man with a quiver of arrows slung on his back and a bow draped over his shoulder squeezed onto the barstool next to him. In fact, he had some trouble getting between the two wide men that were taking up half the bar. It was the only seat left, after all. The man speaking was wearing the armour and mark of Rosewick, so he was obviously a soldier. "We'll have t' fend off the invasion by ourselves I'll bet. No help'll come from the crippled kingdoms of Starbill or Magyther. In fact, we may's well be completely doomed. So mates, 'ave some fun before we all die to the hands of the Tyrans. I 'ear the feast tonight will be a celebration - if King Mortimer is alive, that is - so put on yer best smile fer the ladies." He started to ramble, talking to no-one in particular. "O' course, they'll live. The women and children will be kept as slaves, if I know the Tyrans." The man went on mumbling for a long time, and eventually after grabbing a drink, the younger, sober man sat at a table as far away from the bar - and from the man - as he could get. He gently removed his cloak and placed it on the chair behind him. His face was revealed to be that of the lowly hunter's apprentice, Eric. Animals were once again beginning to appear around the woods near Castle Wormwood, and spring had basically begun. They were all coming out of hibernation, and finally Eric had felt the thud of impact beneath his arrow again. Sat on the opposite side of the table was a stranger he didn't recognise. Their face was hidden underneath a hood and Eric doubted they had any interest in him at all. They only occasionally sipped at a drink of wine. Many others in the inn acted the same way.

Eric stood up as soon as he had drunk a few drinks and immediately returned to his lodge in the woods. Separate to his masters' cabin nearby, it was small - but not tiny. He began his business by grabbing a knife as the sun began to set and strapped on his leather armour, camouflage cape, and green hood. He began into the dark woods that all called the Grayewoods and almost immediately found the tracks of a rabbit, even in the darkness. They seemed fresh and led clear. He followed them only momentarily before he saw a bigger prize: a wild boar. Such meat sold to the butchers for many Gold Roses (the coin of Rosewick). Perhaps if he haggled, he could get up to twenty. And this time he could keep the skin for himself - to decorate his currently bare floor. Previous tries had always resulted in him needing to use his knife, resulting in him ruining the skin of the thing more than an arrow would. His master had a bearskin rug to decorate his floor, but killing such a dangerous creature was not yet the stomach for Eric. But a boar, he could handle. With a silent swish he pulled an arrow from his quiver and nocked it in his birchwood bow. The string, made from the silk of a spider, twanged elegantly as he placed his dart of death into its spot. He drew his bow as far as he could, until the white, slithery chord was tense and could be pulled no longer. He looked on the boar, oblivious to its coming doom, and aimed his bow high. He let his arrow, his death-bullet, loose.

*   *   *

Arora stumbled through the hallways of the castle. It was dark and the torches lining the walls had not yet been lit. In a fit of rage and sadness upon hearing of her husband's death, she had expelled Gallance from the castle, never to return. Halcore would be declared an independent town, no longer a welcome part of Rosewick.

The boar's life quickly ended. The arrow had been fired perfectly; it had pierced straight into the boar through its neck. Eric removed the arrow as soon as the creature was entirely dead, cleaned the wound, then skinned the beast. It was bloody work. He shouldn't have bothered to clean the arrow wound; the entire mat of fur had been stained with blood since then anyway. His job was not entirely neat and it would require washing, but most of the meat had been cut away and he was able to lug his prizes back to his lodge. He would wait till morning to sell the meat and place his new ornament on the floor, but still he was proud. Not yet was he a Master huntsman. He was but an apprentice, and he had killed a boar with a single arrow: a feat even some Masters could not achieve. But it was said that his Master was the best in Rosewick - and rightly so - as he was the Master Huntsman of Castle Wormwood and the villages outside it. No rabbit, boar or bear could escape his Master's tracking; no bandit, no poacher, no lumberjack. He found all that entered the forest, all that disturbed the ancient flow of stillness in the Grayewoods. There were many such disturbances, some far more dangerous than others, and more dangerous than Eric would admit. The job of a huntsman was dangerous, especially as one of the Grayewoods.

*   *   *

Deep in his moody castle in the dull, rainy Halcore, Gallance watched as the flickering, smoky fire continued to rage upon the firewood his servants had scavenged from the forest. The blaze seemed to be in a similar mood to him. He began to think of ways to protect his beloved Rosewick. He could still support the nation of his friend, James II, but could no longer be a strategic advisor of such importance, as he was no longer a part of Queen Arora's Rosewick. What if he were to be the great King of Rosewick? He would be cruel but fair against his enemies, and valiant with his allies. He would be a symbol of the battlefield. King Gallance he could be. He put the thought aside. *I'm too old.* He had no heirs; no-one could succeed him; he had no daughter, no wife. *Unless I rule forever. Unless I simply don't die, which would entail the help of Wizards.* The thoughts of those who practised Magic brought him further into a pit of despair: *Those wraith-touched ones are cursed, and mad beyond measure. Insane men cannot save me.* His own Wizard, his own Wraith-touched, as all large towns and cities had, was useless. His impact on the overall possibilities that Gallance had was extremely small. Before he could conquer immortality, however, Gallance would indeed have to conquer Rosewick. And such a thing he was unprepared to do. He stood from his chair and walked briskly to his study. High bookshelves full of dusty, musty books cornered a small desk where paper, ink and feathers were left. He grabbed a piece of paper and began to write.

"To Duke Henry of Norlick:

As you may already know, King Mortimer of Rosewick died in the North during an assassination attempt on Kaldorn, King-Emperor of half of the world. Our King succeeded in his mission, but was slain after. His body lies in enemy turf. His Queen, Arora, is unstable. In a fit of sadness and rage she expelled me from Castle Wormwood and the Kingdom of Rosewick. It is with pleasure that I secretly announce my desire to be the front of a coup to remove the deranged Queen from power.

You, my friend, have always been my strongest ally other than the late King James. I know you were always scornful of King Mortimer; as was I to a lesser extent - but now he is dead, and we are the most responsible men in the kingdom. Come to my lands, Halcore, and bring all the dukes who you believe would ally with us. If we can gather half or more of the forces of Rosewick, our victory shall be swift - and we shall only reduce the number of soldiers by a few. It is the best choice we can make at this moment in time. Please note I do not wish to kill Arora, only put her out of a position of power in which she could kill us all. "

He sealed the letter with the mark of the Duke of Halcore, then passed the note into the claws of a raven. "Take this to Duke Henry. Show it to no other. He'll be at Castle Wormwood at this moment." The bird began to flutter away in the direction of Castle Wormwood. "The damned bird'll have to go through the Grayewoods. It's unlikely at this time of year that it'll make it." He watched the bird fly away until it disappeared, knowing that the letter the bird carried would impact on the fate of Rosewick. The bird would not arrive till midday the next day he knew, but he was also aware that Duke Henry would make his decision quickly. And it was clear to Gallance what that decision would be.

*   *   *

Eric had sold the boar meat already for eighteen Gold Roses and he hadn't been able to push the price higher. He quietly made his way back to the Grayewoods, where he found his Master's cabin quickly. He entered to find Frederick, his Master, vacant from the first room of the cabin. It was here where he wrote letters, prepared meat, and did many other things. The one place left was his bedroom. It was unlike his Master to sleep till late morning. He knocked upon the wooden door loudly. Groans began to emit from the room, then a shout. "Eric!! I wish you still just waited until I came to get you for training... Wait outside, I'll be ready to hunt in a minute!" Eric left the lodge and waited beside the door. He was a hunter, but also a guardian of the forest. It was only his duty to rid the Grayewoods of dangerous animals, and occasionally kill a few animals in abundance. Of course, it was also his duty to supply the town butcher. As he pondered the true nature of a huntsman's profession, Frederick left the lodge. A second,

12

womanly shape walked out from behind him, shielded from Eric's view by the large, thickly muscled huntsman. "So, Master. You have had a good rest?" As Eric said this, the bigger man chuckled.

"What fine prizes did you find yesterday, if at all?" Asked the larger man.

"Well, boars seem to be in abundance lately. One-arrowed a heavy, fat boar through the neck. Its skin is decorating my floor now."

"So, killing the greatest mammal, the bear, is too daunting a challenge? You're a prodigy, young Eric. Good with a bow as I was a few years ago. To be fair, I killed a bear only in the last two years. At your level I slew a wolf. I decided at the time to wear the thing's skin as a cloak. In fact, it's the one I'm wearing now."

Eric then realised that the grey cloak, perfect for the Grayewoods, was made of matted wolf fur. "How many wolves did you kill? I doubt it only took one to get that much skin."

"Lad, it's best not if you ask how many animals I've killed. I've been hunting for years, and all of my garments are made of cosy fur of some sort, whether it be that of bear, boar or wolf." The huntsman had a grim smile, as if he was ashamed to be prideful of the amount of animals he had slain.

"I reckon, Master, that I am becoming a better bowman daily. In fact, I bet I could shoot a bear to death in one shot. No. A Drake."

"A Drake, huh? Dragon-like creatures too small to qualify as true Dragons - and not immortal like their more powerful cousins - are still big, bigger than bears. Far bigger than us. But to be fair, it has been done before. However, Drakes are ferocious predators - no other tough prey is such a dominating creature, other than Dragons, but I would not call *them* prey - if you encounter them, the scenario reverses, the said Drake or Dragon becoming the dominant predator. However, if you can kill a small bird to show precision and a terrifying bear with bigger teeth, a fiercer temper and an appetite of three times the size to show deadliness, then you can perhaps kill a Drake. I personally think a few more years of hunting could perhaps make you skilled enough to skewer a young Drake."

A raven began to flutter above. "Alright, Eric. Shoot the bird down. Normally, I wouldn't ask such a thing: to kill a feeble bird that can't be eaten; but this is what you wanted, Drake-Bane to-be. " The Master huntsman's simple request was fair. Eric flexed his shoulders back and swiftly pulled an arrow from his quiver to the nock in his bow. He eyed the quick-moving bird briefly. He let his arrow fly through the air. The arrow appeared to be fired too high, but as it sank down lower it appeared (as all of Eric's shots did) to be on perfect trajectory. The unsuspecting raven did not notice the projectile and was not apparent of its wound until it crudely bashed into the hard forest floor that had only just recovered from winter. Eric strode over to his bloody, dead catch from the skies and saw that tied to its feet was a wrapped up letter, and on its curved, creased front was stamped a green and black bear imprisoned in a white circle: the rigid seal of Halcore.

CHAPTER TWO

COUNCIL OF ROSES

"We will need a war plan, Duke Henry. I know you were a strong ally of my father-in-law, a cunning fighter and furthermore, a strategic leader." Queen Arora spoke with a facade of calm, and Henry saw right through the guise. The Queen spoke again, with renewed confidence: "The Tyrans will flow in like boiling magma. They will kill many of us, and the ones only wounded shall be scarred - and rightly so, as we killed their great King-Emperor - but we had to take action. Their beady eye had turned to us midwinter, and they planned to invade in spring. They shall continue with that plan, but I believe that we have another month or two, as their ships must be prepared and the North Sea is wild, dangerous and storm-ridden. They shall have a tough time of it, I believe."

It was the first time Henry had seen her in her stride since the news of King Mortimer's death. Of course, it would not last long - the Queen had intermittent sickness, and he strongly doubted that it would get better - in fact, he had seen himself that it was becoming more and more frequent as time went on.

"Your majesty, if I may. If we have so much time, perhaps it would be best to mobilise the army of Rosewick and all allies it can gather to where the Tyrans are likely to land - their most sensible landing zone among the high cliffs would be the low beach. There is only one area where they could possibly find an easy way to get up to the highlands that we have laid our civilisation upon, that being Torem Coast. It is like a canyon: cliffs are either side. It is easily defendable, and such tactics to defend such a place are easy to decide: and I am certain of the fact that Torem Coast is the answer. If we can gather the kingdoms of Starbill and Magyther, we shall have an indomitable line of defence. Of course, if they are unwise, there are many other places that they could land - but it would make no sense, as it would add months to their travelling time. Torem Coast is the answer."

The Queen considered this momentarily, then spoke, "You do seem sure of yourself, and as such a trusted ally of the crown, I shall take your advise. Perhaps we shall mobilise the army, after I have had council with the rest of the leaders of Rosewick. Such a decision cannot be rushed into. The next council is only a day away - we shall decide then." Duke Henry grimaced, then replied,

"As you wish, your majesty." His answer ended on a cold note. He bowed, then turned and walked with chilled anger out of the throne room. Once again he had been denied leadership - it was probably because he was too close to the exiled Duke of Halcore. However, he strongly believed that the Queen had made a mistake in humiliating him.

*   *   *

Deep in the castle of Vlendale, the King of Starbill displayed a rictus grin at the news.

"Well, well, well. If the beloved King Mortimer of Rosewick has truly fallen, then the indomitable spirit and will of Rosewick shall be faltering. Rosewick will be unable to protect us - it will not even be able to protect itself. We are deeper inland than the kingdom of Roses, and they shall be stampeded first. We, further southward, however, shall be further from the bloodthirsty, brutish Tyrans. For a long period of time. The great Castle Wormwood at the centre of Rosewick is a fortress of great power - if a siege comes, long it shall be. It is good that the Tyrans favour us over the peasants in the pathetic kingdom - perhaps we shall be of more use to them. We are far more exotic. In all ways. Our climate is warmer, paradise to them - our culture and menu more foreign and delicate - yes, we shall be useful. But if it comes to it, I would rather not be a slave to an ugly may-as-well-be-a-jotunn Tyran. Yes. With extra time, we can build protections to our castle - insert rusty metal spikes on our walls, enlist all the warriors that we can muster from all the villages and towns we can reach. Our garrison shall be full and our barracks shall be too. Heh, heh, heh. We shall slay much of their onslaught, and if we do not win - I shall escape before we fall!" A wide, maddened grin spread on his face. The Wraith-Touched king had been having insane fits for years, and yet he still ruled. Many believed he was a pawn of the madly intelligent Prince Isaak, Dragon-Bane of the south. As the people around the king returned to their previous business, the great wooden doors of the throne room were pushed apart, and entered Princess Elaina, daughter of the King. She averted her eyes from the fat man on the throne and the servants around him. The women were cutting his toenails, giving him massages, and combing his hair. The King was mad, and more often than not ignored his servants and preferred to look through the fresco on the ceiling of himself stabbing a dragon. Elaina turned back to him.

"Father, I heard you had received important news. What information did you gain?" She spoke with near-unnatural grace and elegance.

"My sweet daughter," he said, having one of his lucid moments. "The King of Rosewick is dead, as is Kaldorn, King-Emperor of the Tyrans."

*   *   *

In the barracks of Castle Wormwood, soldiers gossiped as they took off their armour. "Well, I heard that the Queen is going to mobilise the army. That being us, and many others." said one soldier.

"Hah! I heard that the Queen is so fat with pregnancy, that she can't mobilise at all!" replied another one, just as he heaved off his helmet. As they took off their armour, all their faces and chests were revealed to be gleaming with globules of sweat. Most of the greasy bodies were bloodied and bruised.

"Let's just be glad that the training session is over. Battlemaster Voss seemed to be in a bad mood. If we chattered now, he'd probably punish us with another day of duelling." The one with the styled brown hair seemed to be the most sensible, the least sweaty and the least bloody.

A far larger and sweatier soldier spoke.

"Thomas, you bloody bugger. Duelling ain't a bloody' punishment fer you. You did the bloody best - very, very bloody, in fact. You made all of us bloody. Voss put us in one by one, and we all fell. You steamrolled thru' us, you did. An' we paid. Made us look pathetic, you did. Maybe even ruined our careers." The man was only wearing a chestplate and armoured leggings, and had taken his gauntlets, helmet and boots off. He began to glare at the other, more muscular man. He then glanced away to the other soldiers in the room, looking for allies. Thomas walked over to the rude, insolent speaker and grabbed him by his chestplate. "Ah, shit. This is the one time armour doesn't help me. I'm agile and stronger while naked. Many know that." The man about to be hurt smiled. A few around the room chuckled at this, but most remained silent while Thomas lifted the man, whose resistance had been broken, off the ground. The brute began to brace for impact, then was head-butted. Blood began to froth out of his mouth as he was thrown to the floor. Thomas sat on his bruised body and began to punch his face senseless. When Thomas was pulled up by a few soldiers behind him, he cleared his throat, and continued to pull off the rest of his armour while resuming his sitting on a bench. The body on the floor remained there, unmoving and unconscious. The thing's eyes were closed. The soldiers dressed back into the clothes they had left in the room before, and left the room, a few of them cooperatively dragging the senseless pile of flesh, sweat and blood with them.

*   *   *

"Alright, Eric," said Frederick as he brandished the letter from Halcore, "Don't tell anyone about this. The letter speaks of treachery against our Queen. But I'm not sure if it's an entirely bad thing. Go out and enjoy the rest of your day. I must ponder this a while longer, and read it through a few more times. The overall message is puzzling, and some of it is bloodstained. I must make sense of it. I will tell you my decision tomorrow morning."

"But -"

"No buts, Eric. Nobody can know."

*   *   *

When the soldiers from the barracks arrived outside the castle, they found a few others waiting for them. By then the man who had been beaten up - his name was Louis - had once again come to his senses. He was still grumbling. A shape suddenly appeared alongside the soldiers. It spoke, "So guys, what did Voss put you through this time?" asked the shape in grey fur. The top of his cloak had the skin of a wolf head attached to it as a hood.

"Hey!! Eric, where'd you get the wolf-fur! Did you pin a wolf to a tree, like you'd always wanted to?" asked a soldier named Edward loudly. It seemed that he had already found something to drink.

"Nahhh, borrowed it from my Master."

"A shame, a shame. Which tavern will run out of ale tonight?"

Louis giggled.

"Why not the Hung Crows's Inn? I've got some… heh… business… there."

"Well, why not the Hung Crow's Inn? I think all our favourite watering holes are out of water!!" shouted another shadowy shape without thought. A few more laughs and "Aye"s confirmed the Hung Crow's Inn, and the party began to walk on through the village surrounding Castle Wormwood.

When they arrived after only ten minutes of walking at the Hung Crow's Inn, they found it was bustling. They only barely managed to find seats for all of them, and the table was the one furthest from the bartender. Eric stood after briefly sitting.

"And what shall you all be having, er… gentlemen?" he asked, clearly unsure of them due to their sweaty and bloody appearance.

"What else is there to have than the bloody drinks, stale bread and poisoned soup? I'll have a bottle o' wine." responded beaten Louis.

"Ruuughhh….. Mugga ale, thanks Eric." Edward had already drunk a bottle of ale he had found in the castle, and was lost in thought. Everyone else leaned towards ale as well, and soon all of their breaths smelt inebriated, and all were drunk.

"You reckon I have a chance with the barmaid o'er there?" asked Edward some time later. Louis had long since disappeared in the company of a feminine figure, and the rest of the soldiers were beginning to leave as well. Edward had no response, and soon it was just he, Thomas and Eric left. "Ah, why not pick a fight with some idiots, make ourselves look good an' then get the attention I bloody well think's worth it of that barmaid. An' maybe you guys'll get summin' outta it as well." Edward said this even more drunkenly than he was. Then, Thomas said, "Alright then." The muscular young man was up from his chair in seconds, and walked away into a corner. "What is Thomas doing?" Eric hissed to Edward, who had collapsed his face into his drink. Another new man, seeing the open spot, sat down. Then, Thomas returned.

"Allo allo what do we 'ave here. You took me buggerin' seat!!" The man who had only just sat down turned to Thomas behind him in fear.

"But… You weren't sitting in it."

"I was sitting in it before, you chair thief. I'll break your skull for that bloody chair! The chair's worth more than your head and all in your purse, mate! I'll have you know I'm a soldier of Rosewick, and if you don't believe me…. That's another reason to embellish this chair with your bones." The other man stood, apologised, then left the bar unscathed, although he had to run to escape Thomas's vengeful punch. The rest of the evening was forgotten by Edward, Eric and Thomas, and none of the other drunkards of the bar could hope to tell the story either.

"It pleases me to see you all here today. As you may already know, my husband, King Mortimer, is dead. But remember this - he succeeded on the mission he set out to do, and slew Kaldorn, who shall never trouble us again. But the Tyrans shall come for vengeance once winter has ended - they shall arrive with their axes in only a few months - and we must prepare plans. Duke Henry has told me that Torem Coast shall likely be their landing zone. All who agree say Aye!" before responses came to Queen Arora, there was a light murmuring in the room. "Aye!!" shouted the majority of the audience. The ones who didn't seemed in a bad mood. Then, one spoke:
"What is your view on it, your majesty?" asked the Duke of Oldale.

"I believe personally that Torem Coast shall be our destination, and that we should mobilise and set up armaments and fortifications immediately." replied Arora.

"I strongly agree with our Queen, men. It is the best strategical option of ours, and the Tyrans will not see such resistance coming." Duke Henry's voice raised over the din of all, dominating the room and forcing the others into silence.

"We came here with such urgency to discuss this one issue. This council is now at its end." with the Queen's last words of the council, all began to rise and exit the room.

*   *   *

Prince Isaak snarled in the face of his father, King Vorodin.

"You're telling me what now? Crop failure due to drought? This bodes terribly for our already minimal chance of fighting off the Tyrans. If it comes to a war of attrition now, we shall starve. Father, this does not bode well at all." Prince Isaak looked back to his father, who was gibbering with insanity.

Princess Elaina came into the room.

"Isaak. It is getting worse. I came here earlier and he had been insane for hours before I came. I am still wondering if the Wraith's touch was meant to kill him, but Destiny decided that Father was still needed. Have you heard the news of your friend, King Mortimer?"

"He has returned from the North?"

"He killed Kaldorn." the awkwardness between the two siblings was obvious.

"Incredible. Such a brutal fighter… But what indeed happened to Mortimer? If it is horrifying, then my need to know is doubled."

"Mortimer is dead in the North, and Queen Arora shall not even have his body for the funeral."

The only two children of Starbill's monarch turned to their mad father, both knowing what was to come. "Someday Father shall die. Destiny has plans for him, and he has done nothing since he was Touched other than scream and talk." Elaina had already accepted the fact that King Vorodin would die.

"Destiny is cruel, sister."

"If you choose to believe that he could ever possibly recover, then you are as insane as he, brother. You shall never learn, and when you become King, you will be the one to sit idly on the throne, screaming like a newborn and staring into the stars."

*   *   *

Eric awoke with a terrible hangover and could barely stand from his bed. A gruelling headache filled his skull with pain. His teeth felt like they had grown fur. His stomach ached as much as his face had after he first bantered with Thomas. He left his bedroom, dressed in his criss-crossed jacket and jeans, grabbed his bow, a quiver of arrows and was then ready. He left the cabin he called home and walked a few metres to the entrance of his Master's, where he found a note pinned to the door.

"Going to speak to Duke Henry. Don't wait for me, Eric. Grab a few rabbits and meet me at the training grounds when the sun first appears above the trees." Eric obeyed his master's commands, slowly recovering from his hangover, which was greatly impacting on his skill with a bow. His hands were shaking when he held his long, stretchy string and when he let his arrow fly he moved at the last second, thus ruining his shot and telling his prey of his presence. When he did first hit something other than the ground in the forest, it was a tree. Stumbling grumpily through the forest after failing miserably repeatedly at hunting, he realised the sun was beginning to peak through the trees. He was running out of time. He hurriedly rushed along, taking in no note of his surroundings. He even failed to notice the cave and the rocks on the ground that he tripped on. He fell brutally backwards onto the ground, a few jagged rocks cutting a thick scratch in his right arm, then realising he had pinned his left arm underneath his whole weight, at an awkward angle as well. The pain began to arrive, filling his arm up to the brim and spilling into his shoulder. He cursed loudly than he ever had before when he pulled his limp arm from under him, and another spasm of pain arched across him. But what he was far, far more concerned about was the thumping echoing from inside the cave. He could only see shallowly in and even then it was dark, but he could hear something big and heavy coming through the cave. With fear, he then cursed:

"It's a bloody bear."

CHAPTER THREE

THE GATHERING

"I am glad you received my message, Duke Henry. And I am even further pleased by the fact you have brought half of the power of Rosewick here with you. And they all agree with our cause?" Duke Gallance asked with a serpentine smile.

"My friend, all here were appalled at the power that has been given to the Queen, but I must speak to you alone after this meeting. There is something important to be discussed about the message you sent me. Anyway, continue." replied Henry.

"My friends, we shall see the fall of Queen Arora and the rise of something far greater: King Gallance Of Rosewick! All we must do is secure the throne from a pregnant, mourning lady. Such an easy task can be done by some of the greatest leaders in all South." exclaimed Gallance grandly.

A few shouts screamed through the morning air. Gallance was surprised to see most of them so involved and excited. He caught one or two malicious looks directed at him, and eyes were flickering between Duke Henry and he. There were half a dozen of the dukes of Rosewick in addition to Duke Gallance and Duke Henry, and Gallance began to feel outnumbered. But after a relaxed evening of planning and drinking, the feeling had slipped away. The guests filtered out of his home before midnight, and finally he was able to speak to Duke Henry alone.

"What did you wish to speak to me about, Henry?"

"Your messenger bird was shot down by a huntsman's apprentice. Name was Eric or something. His Master, the greatest Hunter in all Rosewick, brought the letter to me after the Council of Roses. I came here with allies as quickly as I could. Some earls, others dukes, some barons - but all leaders. We know that his Master is a supporter of ours, or he would have told the Queen and an army would be marching to us right now. But we have no idea of his apprentice."

"Then surely this huntsman's apprentice is a target for us."

"Indeed, Gallance. This could prove dire for us."

"I shall send a troop of soldiers there, Duke Henry. He shall be eliminated. There will be no way we, great Dukes, could be implicated or proven guilty."

"Exactly."

"Servant! Come here. Rouse Sir Rusga and tell him he is needed."

"Duke Gallance. When you come to be King, I shall be glad to serve you." said King Henry. In the relative darkness, Gallance could not see the facade of cunning behind Duke Henry's simple, innocent smile. The two men chatted further awhile, then a huge form of metal and muscle entered through the door. It was Sir Rusga.

"My lords. What is your command, sire?" The hulking knight seemed to be a brute. Such a thing was uncommon among the knights of the South - brutish tendencies were more common amongst Tyrans - yet he was as much a citizen of Torem as any other.

"Sir Rusga, take a troop of your men to the Grayewoods, and eliminate the huntsmen who work there. If possible, slay only the apprentice. The master could be… useful… to us. Leave the body, it must be discovered. I have a great plan, now." Duke Gallance's command seemed to please the giant in armour.

"At once, my Lord. And his name?"

"Eric. He has no surname. Make sure he dies. Do not bring him in as a captive or I shall make you ride out there alone and slay him at the Grayewoods."

"My lord, I find never bother with the consequences of taking captives. It is better to behead them on the field."

"Your mercilessness is already well known by both of us, Rusga. Now go."

"Yes, sire. Blood shall stain the forest floor, of Eric Null-House and perhaps of his master. Dice of death shall be thrown, and at the wishing of the Duke Of Halcore."

Rusga left the room, and as the door slowly closed and heavy footsteps trumpeted away, Henry unsheathed his dagger, and slid the sharp point of his dagger up Gallance's throat, who fell to floor, his blood staining the rug crimson red. The Duke Of Halcore - Gallance - was dead.

*   *   *

"So... we're being mobilised alongside the rest of the soldiers. To Torem Coast." it would be the first battle that Thomas, Edward and Louis fought in.

"We'll crush the enemy. Those Tyrans have no idea what's coming to them."

"Mate. Louis. Some Tyrans are twice your size. And you think we'll 'crush' them? Each monster shall take down a few of us."

"Then it shall just have to be us that do not fall! None shall fell us!"

"Your optimism is always inspiring, Louis." the sarcastic note of Thomas' voice once again pierced the ears of Louis and Edward.

"As foot soldiers, we're almost entirely doomed to be trampled. I heard they didn't have many horses up North, but still - our allies will not care if they trample a few pathetic men in bloody armour wielding bent swords." Edward seemed in an even more sour mood than usual.

"Exactly, Edward. You are all doomed to die in the coming battle. To think I'd taught you so well!" the impressive, hulking shape of Battlemaster Voss appeared behind them. The incredible warrior was the half-brother of perhaps the most brutal warrior of the South, Sir Rusga.

"In fact, I can confirm your deaths to you now. You're all being enlisted to the front line! As a part of the group of suicidal men to attack the Tyrans as they charge up Torem Coast, you're certain to at least be wounded. But even our main strategist, Duke Henry, admitted that you're likely to die."

He saluted them and walked away. "Is it true then, that we'll be charging the Tyrans?" it was Louis who asked the question.

"Likely. Voss is exactly the kind of person to engineer his least favourite students into being slain."

"Well, the entire army is being gathered outside Castle Wormwood at midday. Then we'll all march to Torem Coast."

*   *   *

Eric fell to his knees as the huge bear half-emerged from its shadowy cave. It quickly and aggressively approached its limp target, moving in for a bite. Eric, used to the dextrous aiming of a bow, swung to the side of the bear's jaw just in time. He drew his knife with his one good arm and brought it forth in front of his body. He would be unlikely to survive the battle. He stabbed it into the bear's thick, matted fur, sending blood flying. The bear appeared not to notice the cut from the blade, and brought its jaws down on Eric's unprotected shoulder. The human yelped and dug his blade further into the bear's sinewy flesh, gouging out chunks of animal. It was with these terrible injuries that the bear became enraged with Eric, and began to tear up his already limp arm. Pain sliced clean through any coherent thought that Eric could gather, and frenzy came over him. A battlecry sourced from nowhere escaped his mouth in a howl, then he began to grip around the bear's neck with both hands. It flexed its clamp of spikes down to chew upon his finger and tore it straight off. Missing his index finger was extremely painful and the morsel of food the bear devoured was not returned. Taking no heed of his pain, he began to squeeze. Harder and harder until his hands ached. The bear stopped its incessant attacking with its tearing teeth as its head was snapped backwards. It pawed at Eric with ravaging claws in a final attempt to survive, but as its head was torn backwards from its body, its eyes turned lifeless and its deadweight flopped to the floor. Eric stood, holding his limp arm to his body. Blood stung his eyes from where the bear had had blood frothing from its mouth, and the mess around Eric was terrible. But as he heard a voice calling his name, the world faded around him and he fell to the stone. The darkness was welcomed.

"Ah, good. You are awake."

"Master?" Eric's first words since he had fainted were croaky.

"Yes, it is I. I have treated your injuries and I tore the bear's head off so you can mount it on your wall. Nothing else of its body could possibly have be cleaned of all that blood. And you. Your arm was out of its socket and your shoulder was mangled - you lost a finger and a chunk of your arm is missing. In fact, you did pretty well."

"Hmmpphh…. The bear didn't dislocate my arm. That was me falling half into the cave and pinning my arm underneath myself."

"You were near death, I believe. It was a miracle you survived. The only reason I found you was that shouting scream of a battle cry you let rip across the woods. Sounded like a Tyran's!" Eric was surprised to see his Master joking with him straight after an injury.

"Master, what news comes from the Castle? Do they march yet?" the question was genuine.

"They have been marching for two hours, Eric. Your friends came by and told me some news. They're not likely to come back, I'm afraid. That Battlemaster Voss of theirs engineered them into being part of the group of foot soldiers who attack the charging Tyrans as they advance up Torem Coast."

"They're clearly doomed, then." Eric's face was blank. His master turned and went out of Eric's cabin. He closed the door, then there was a thud, then, a heavy smash as if a body had fallen to the ground. Eric stood, grabbed his bow, a quiver of arrows his Master had left by the door, and rushed out of the cabin. There, outside was his Master on the ground. He had been punched by a huge man in armour next to him, who prepared to grab Eric - but missed. Eric began to run, however he quickly realised he was surrounded and not entirely recovered from his injuries. *Why attack huntsmen?* The thought then made Eric realise he was in a battle once again. He barged past one of the armoured men, shoving him to the side as strongly as he could. It hurt his arm, but the man was pushed backwards and stumbled into a tree. His helmet clanged and a look of anger came across his face. He began to make chase but as everyone knows, armour was not made for running contests. The rest of the knights followed suit, and began to run. Eric was much faster in his lighter leather armour and as they fell further and further behind, he pulled an arrow from his quiver and quickly shot a single attempt at the huge man who he now recognised as Sir Rusga, a knight of Halcore. The arrow pierced into his armour but the knight was indifferent to the damage. It seemed he felt no pain. Eric turned his attention to the other men. *Surely they would have arrived on horseback?* But then he saw the horses left in the forest up ahead of him. *The fools should not have left the horses where I could have gotten to them!* He grinned and leapt up onto the unfamiliar mane. He hoped it was not a steed loyal to its master.

"Hiya!" Upon Eric's saying of the word, the horse began to gallop through the forest. As soon as his pursuers reached the horses, all but one clambered on to their steeds. The last was left behind. Rusga shouted, "Guard the other Huntsman! We'll get this one!" and then the one left behind was left with a purpose.

"Yes, Sir Rusga."

*   *   *

A small servant came in and whispered to Prince Isaak of Starbill, then left the room once again.

"Rosewick marches. This is disturbing," said Prince Isaak at the arrival of the news from Rosewick, "A line of defence best played at Castle Wormwood has been cast to the point where the Tyrans shall be strongest. However, if they had lain in wait further along the enemy's warpath, then bandits and environmental conditions would have further weathered the invaders down. However, they have chosen to eliminate the bandits as they march and clear such obstacles. Such a strategic decision could only have been made by a mastermind with a plan to turn the situation around. I could only expect warriors who fought side-by-side with James II to think of such a plan." The room was filled simply with a long table and chairs, but only two sat there on either end. The Prince and the Princess both had wine cups, fancy gold goblets, full of red liquid. Their plates had dormant food, untouched, decorating them.

"Brother, you do not understand how clear this is. The Dukes of Rosewick seek to wrest the throne of Castle Wormwood from the hands of Queen Arora. It is exactly what they would do and exactly what I would expect of that recently exiled Duke Gallance." Princess Elaina looked scornfully upon her brother.

"It matters not who rules Rosewick. The kingdom is inevitably a shield between us and the Tyrans." said Isaak.

"Your heart is spectacularly cold, brother," responded Elaina, "To think you could call human lives a 'shield' between the enemy and yourself is one of your more *brilliant* works, I must say. I am glad our Father has loved; for a good King has loved and is a lover of its people. You, my chilling sibling, have not loved. And along this slippery, icy slope of your heart you shall never love nor be loved." The comment barely stung through the frozen snow that built the Prince's chest and had no visible effect upon his expression.

"Sister, if a monarch wept every time one of their people died, then they would spend their lives weeping. It is pointless to be sorrowful over a fallen scullion or a long-lived chambermaid - they are plentiful, replaceable, and all of them are the same."

"You should weep, brother, for your own winter soul. But your tears shall be blades of ice because your heart is so cold, and sting your eyes. When your eyes are wet, your eyes are frozen over. Your shouts echo like avalanches

41

between mountains, bringing only cold and death. When one seeks warmth but you are the only one left, they do not approach you - for your blood runs like icy streams slicing fields coated in snow from each other, separating things meant to be together. You are a bitter wraith, a spirit only of ice and wickedness."

"I know you shall leave tonight, sister. All I have to say is that the castle shall no longer be plagued by the likes of you. All shall be glad and merriments shall spread," he spat, "And keep in mind a lesson: those you attack shall counter." Upon saying this he threw his cup of wine, which clanged against her arm. In the same way the verbal attacks could not harm her brother, it seemed this mighty toss had not even grazed Elaina. She turned and left the room. She was quiet but both knew it had been an argument in her favour. Now, all she needed to do was to prepare to flee the castle, she was certain an 'unfortunate' accident would happen to her if she stayed.

*   *   *

The army had made camp a mile off from Torem Coast for the night, and Duke Henry had already risen. A few knights accompanied him. The guards outside the

Queen's tent had already been slain, the only two victims the Duke hoped the coup would claim, and had been slain brutally. It was a downside that Duke Henry could not let distract him. He barged into the Queen's tent. He sneered, then spoke with disdain:

"My Queen, it is with regret that I announce that you are no more the monarch of Rosewick. I may now call you Arora. You are pathetic; your stomach has grown bigger and you are sick. You are indeed not in a fit state to rule. Thus I have taken responsibility. Mobilising the army has put you into a tent and with only two guards, and I have been positioned near you. Your compliance to my idea was wonderfully stupid."

"Henry… Treachery?"

"It has come to it, yes. You are not in a fit state to rule. You are mourning your husband's death and carrying his child. Adding the burden of ruling a kingdom is not good for your health. You must rest."

"I would have expected Gallance of such a deed, but you? You were trusted."

"Arora, it was always I who was more scornful of your husband. King Mortimer's bravado in going to the North and dying was the perfect opportunity to save James II's kingdom. In fact, I have saved the South."

"No, you have betrayed your Queen, the late King, and his father. You should be spat on, Henry. To think you were trusted…" Arora was disgusted.

"Alas, Arora, a King is not spat upon in his own lands. I should think not!! Such disrespect from the people he rules over! Terrible, I must say," he began his speech, "That you should lose control. But I shall not kill you. I shall allow your child to spring forth into the world… And I shall leave you alive. But if you dare make a move against me, your head shall spring from your neck and your children shall be banished, to live eternally as peasants, not knowing of their royal blood."

"And if you had failed here?" asked Arora.

"Well, my second plan would spill far more blood than this one, I can confirm," said he, "But that knowledge is not yours. For Arora, you have been ousted."

*   *   *

Frederick felt his eyes flutter, then they stayed themselves. He began to focus on his surroundings. He was tied to his cabin. One of the armoured men he had briefly seen before blacking out watched him, and began strutting over.

"It shall be fun to watch you die. Your death shall be far more enjoyable now that you are awake. I was beginning to lose patience." Fred would have responded, but he found that his mouth was indeed bound.

"I think I'll hang you from that tree." He pointed to the big oak that had been there for thousands of years. "And if your neck proves sturdy, I'll just cut down the tree to smash onto your cabins. NNnnnnnnn… Actually, haven't searched 'em yet…" he came out ten minutes later with the bag of gold coins Fred kept in his draw. "You've actually got some coin, 'avent you. Killin' a rich man!" Me mates'll be happy." Fred spat away the rope in his mouth easily, then spoke.

"You're not a knight."

"Do you expect me to be? I tagged along on this mission. Replaced another guy whose body is buried in the wilds east of here. I abducted him myself. I wore his armour, they thought I was he, then I saw this golden opportunity: two houses, an' ready for pillaging. And you were wondering who I was? Givvit a guess, sir!"

"You are a bandit. Simple."

"Aw, how'd ya guess? I was gonna kill ya if yer guessed wrong."

"So now you're not going to kill me."

"You make me angry, sir. I won't kill ya, I'll just cause you to die! I'll make sure those ropes are nice 'n' tight, then I'll leave ya out to the crows! I'm nit quite the dullest either, good sir." He walked over and began pulling at the ropes, making sure they were tight. He pulled one near Fred's arm, and he did not expect the consequences. Fred's arm snaked out of the opening and thwapped into a fist. The closed ball was thrust forwards and mashed into the bandit's stomach. With his free arm he loosened his ropes and freed himself. Fred drew his knife from his belt - the stupid bandit had left it within reach - and the bandit drew an equally long and sharp weapon from his boot. "Game on, sir. We'll see who'll have a slit throat and who'll be livin'."

CHAPTER FOUR

MUTINY OF THE SHORES

Edward was aghast, "Henry has taken control of Rosewick? The Duke Henry? The one who accompanied Duke Gallance and James II into valiant battle? He's middle-aged, cunning, still a good warrior, strong - but he certainly has a wicked streak. When a group of feral Goblins encountered him in the woods, their heads were being hung on stakes outside his fortress only hours later. He is bloodthirsty against the Tyrans, he hated King Mortimer. No man could be a worse King, save perhaps Battlemaster Voss, who almost certainly schemed with Henry."

The news of the successful coup had already reached Thomas, Louis, Edward and the rest of the soldiers who trained with them.

"But as soldiers, shouldn't we have tried to help defend the Queen? It surely would have been our duty to behead Henry."

"Indeed, Edward. But the bloody Henry has far more support than the Queen ever had, and the supporters of the Queen have all disappeared." Thomas's mind was level-headed.

"Thomas. We should bloody fight! If we're gonna die, we may as well die to allies. I'd rather not give Voss his satisfaction of causing our deaths himself." responded Louis.

"That reason is almost enough, Louis. Our blood is boiling for a fight. And we shall have one - but if we weaken our own troops even before the Tyrans arrive, Rosewick shall be even more hopeless than any ever believed. In fact, I can guarantee that in this situation we shall die. 'Tis fate."

"Optimism is the answer! We can begin our own coup. We can plan well, we're not the dullest of soldiers, an' we can fight as well! 'Tis known well you are a barbaric fighter, too, Thomas. We have opportunities, and if we were to give the Queen back her power, then think of the rewards and prizes we may receive! And if perhaps we are given knighthoods, to new levels of nobility we shall rise! Then, if the Queen has a daughter, our sons would be excellent suitors and then monarchs would have sprung from our loins!"

"An impressive imagination you have, Louis," Thomas stood over the other man and grabbed his face. "But Louis, three men cannot oust a King. Planning and support is required, furthermore we shall not be given a scarce moment to prepare."

"Ah, but the coup has only just occurred! Guards would not yet be positioned outside Henry's tent. With stealth, we can destroy him! It must be done tonight." Edward was caught up in Louis's optimism.

"Fine, men. But we shall go in on my lead." Thomas immediately grabbed the position of leader.

*   *   *

The thumping of horseshoes was now imprinted in Eric's head. He had perhaps gone deeper into the Grayewoods than he ever had before; the dark groves were maddening his mind. *No! I shall not fall to weakness!* He was being pursued by only one rider now, one he thought he could make out as Sir Rusga. The few arrows he fired at the brute simply twanged off his armour. It seemed Eric would have to focus his aim and fire with far more precision. But then, even as trained as it was, the horse Eric was riding stumbled as it dashed through thorny bushes, then half tripped on a root of a tree. Eric was thrown off, the undergrowth slicing his clothes and scratching his skin. He cowered in the bushes only a moment longer till he stood, stayed his soul, drew his bow, raised his arm to take an arrow, took an arrow, brought the arrow to the nock of his bow, pulled the string back and - finally - released. The arrow reached the daunting hulk that was too stupid to wear a helmet, then pierced the enraged eye of Sir Rusga. A deep, vile scream echoed through the Grayewoods. Three more arrows quickly followed, taking the horse down and pinning its master to the floor. The horse, not seriously injured, raised itself from the ground, then trampled the body and sped away. Rusga was not dead, but he had been knocked unconscious.

Eric's destination would be Torem Coast; it made sense if the soldiers of Halcore were attacking him, he did know of Duke Gallance's plan to hold a coup. His Master would be fine. If Gallance had not been stopped before Eric reached Torem Coast, then he would attempt to prevent it, unless it had already happened. And Eric suspected that the movement of the coup would be swift. Eric mounted his horse once again minutes later and fled the scene; he was sure that Rusga would wake up eventually, as long as he remained unharmed by the creatures of the Grayewoods.

*   *   *

Arora was writing. It was difficult to hide the letter from her guards, but it was manageable. King Mortimer had had a friend: Prince Isaak of Starbill. She was not so keen on the Prince herself, but she knew very well that the Princess, his sister Elaina, was elegant, beautiful, kind, cunning and had command of some of the people of Starbill. And that Arora could definitely rely upon.

"Dear Princess Elaina,

I have been ousted. Duke Henry - or now, King Henry - has plotted against me. I am in desperate need of your help. Soon I will be unable to travel far. I am being held currently with the army at Torem Coast. Come to me quickly, I shall return the favour someday if you help.

- Arora"

She sent the message via one of her non-imprisoned handmaidens who was allowed to visit her. The girl was brave and had fearlessly left for Starbill. Arora strongly doubted that she would fail her mission. And if she did, then that meant she was dead. She would complete the mission or die trying. Little did Arora know that Princess Elaina had already travelled miles from Vlendale, the capital of Starbill and the home of Prince Isaak, King Vorodin and Princess Elaina.

*   *   *

Princess Elaina rode. She had stolen the best horse from the royal stables and had escaped during the night. No guards had been in her escape route; it was obvious that her brother had allowed her to leave. She had been riding for a day since then. Elaina would go to Rosewick to see Queen Arora, and if she could, help strategise against the incoming Tyrans. She had encountered no trouble yet, but was beginning to reach the nearest town from the capital of Starbill - Murlith. It wasn't big or important enough to hold anyone who would immediately recognise her. In fact, she reasoned that it would be safe - *but a disguise,* she thought - *may be necessary.*

She arrived at the town shortly before the sun had set, and found a reasonable tavern within minutes - Murlith was known for the amount of drunkards it housed and the beer its bartenders served. It seemed a relatively unpopular place. She bought no drinks but did buy the finest room they had. She paid him a few coins from her purse and inconspicuously immediately went up to her room. All who saw her didn't give her a second thought, she blended right in. The room, in fact, turned out to be disgusting. The floorboards were coated with dust and muck, the beams in the ceiling had rats and dying bugs crawling across them at all times, the window was half shattered, thus the floor near there was wet, the roof had gaps and thus had water dripping into buckets which had been placed on the ground. All buckets were nearly full as it was raining, and one was fully loaded and beginning to spill over. The bed itself was the cleanest part - it was slightly wet and the structure was mouldy. Otherwise, it was fine. She managed to sleep in the cold, wet and disgusting room but her sleep did not last long and she had disappeared from the town by the time the bartender had opened the tavern again. She made it across the border that morning, and for the rest of the day she was glad that the huge fortress of Vlendale was near the border between Starbill and Rosewick. It had made her journey far, far easier.

*   *   *

"Elaina has disappeared. Excellent. Now she cannot stand in the way."

"Stand in the way of what, your majesty?"

"My father shall not recover from this madness. But what we can do is fake his death: send him East across the sea to that vile place we shall not name, then I take the throne. This useless King can no longer be coped with."

"I do agree, your majesty. And if my service at all is required, I shall be ready." the Prince's right hand, the rat-ish fellow named Niurmuc, was a shadowy figure among the nobles and all would not be surprised if he turned out to be a thief or assassin. But his loyalty to the Prince was certain, everyone knew that, but nobody except the Prince could trust him. His gray eyes surveyed the room, watching the servants. The Prince spoke again. "Leave us, servants." The four servants left the room obsequiously.

"Thank you, your majesty. I appreciate this one-to-one opportunity. In fact, I have matters that I do need to speak of with you."

"And?" the Prince was getting impatient.

"My spies have found information. You do know your dead friend's wife, Queen Arora?"

"Yes... Why?"

"Of course. She no longer bears the title of Queen. Duke Henry has taken ahold of Rosewick."

"Duke Henry? That savage bastard tore through the armies of Starbill when I was young! He assaulted us all and he killed my mother! That son-of-a-goblin has made his way to the throne? This is not a laughing matter. Arora and Mortimer we could indeed trust, as they were my friends and my strong allies. But, alas, a nobleman who hated them both and hated us even more has taken charge. He shall wage war on us at the first opportunity!"

"Indeed. I believe it may be in our best interest to... stir... things up." Niurmuc's face sprouted a bloodthirsty smile.

*　　　*　　　*

The knife ripped through Fred's leather armour and only caused a minor scratch on his skin. It was his turn to act. He attempted to rip his knife through the bandit, trying to cut him in half. But he failed, and only jammed his knife into the crotch of his enemy, who screamed in pain. Blood began to stream from the wound.

"You fat bastard! I'll slit your throat fer that one!" The sly-talking bandit had quickly become a shouting lunatic in the bloody fight. Little blood was staining the Master ranger's armour, however. It was the shear vitality of the bandit that was keeping the fight going. Most would be dead if they had lost the amount of blood he had, but somehow he had survived. Fred ducked as the bandit leapt at him, knife in hand. The knife went straight over the huntsman, and the bandit's chest was thrust forwards to Fred's knife. He took the opportunity and stabbed through the thick flesh, creating a jagged hole in the bandit's fleshy, muscular chest. Too disgusted with the sight to take the blood-coated knife out of the gaping, bloody hole in the bandit's chest (which was quickly filling up with even more blood), he left the weapon to rust in the corpse's liquids. After burying the body in the woods, he put bandages on his own injuries, he grabbed a quiver of arrows and his bow, and began tracking the hoofmarks of many horses through the forest. They lead far and wide, and he found many bodies and dead horses along the way. He was glad that none of the corpses belonged to Eric. It seemed his apprentice had survived. He came past Sir Rusga, who he could only assume was dead, as his breathing and heartbeat were almost nonexistent, but if the huntsman noticed he was alive, he took no action upon the fact. He was indeed impressed with the arrow that had embedded itself in the knight's eye and knew without a doubt that wherever Eric had gone, Fate had chosen for him to be there. So the master huntsman stopped following the tracks of his apprentice, and returned to his lodge. Peace was there again in the Grayewoods.

*   *   *

Thomas, Edward and Louis approached the large tent slowly. They had been creeping for half an hour, and had not yet been noticed. So, so far they had called their mission 'successful'. But it was the next part of their mission that would be the hardest. "Pssst! Guys! I had an amazing idea! We set his tent on fire."

"You are dull, Edward. The fire would spread and kill far more than we would have intended. And we would unlikely kill Henry with that act. And if we were discovered, we would be a thousand times more likely to be executed. If Henry wakes while we are trying to kill him, we'll still probably be able to kill him. If he's outnumbered, we should be fine. Now, Edward. Poke your head under the tent to see whether he is awake or not."

The man poked his head under, then said: "Well, he's awake. But he's absent minded while looking blankly into a mirror while trying on a crown."

"How the bloody hell could you see in the bloody dark?"

"Me mum always makes carrot soup for lunch. An' dinner. Heard carrots help sight. Course, carrots are all we eat at me mum's farm. She's a carrot farmer. That means I eat carrots for every meal. Gets me eyesight very good."

"Edward, where'd you find that bottle of ale?" Thomas watched as Edward took a swig from a bottle.

"Took it from a barrel earlier. Remember where I held you guys up for a moment? That was me getting me a drink." Edward gave a half-smile to his companions.

"Gimme, you selfish bastard." Louis reached over and snatched the bottle from the slightly inebriated man's grip.

"Alright. Let's sneak in under here. Avoid being spotted via the mirror. Be silent. Or we'll die." said Thomas. They all went under the tent edge to crawl across the floor. Thomas silently drew his dagger, then mouthed to the other two "I'll stab him first, then you guys surround 'im."

Clumsily, Louis dropped his bottle on the floor in an attempt to grab his dagger. It loudly smashed into a thousand pieces, shattering all over the floor and spraying shards of glass into his face. It didn't seem his eyes were splashed, however. "Almighty Lord of the Afterlife. Give us divine intervention." Thomas' prayer seemed to be a desperate last hope. Henry turned to the three men behind him, who all stood up.

"Welcome, gentlemen." In a flash, he drew his sword and had knocked his hilt to Edward's nose. Edward had fallen to the floor in moments face-down, his nose beginning to bruise and bleed and his cheek being impaled by a shard of glass.

"What indeed is your business here?" asked Henry slowly.

Thomas and Louis fumbled with their swords and drew them after Henry had waited for a moment.

"Ah. I see you truly are gentlemen. All of us do like a good, fair, bloody fight." an unpleasant smile slowly curled into reality on Henry's lips.

* * *

Eric was riding quickly. He was getting closer to his goal, Torem Coast. He had been riding all afternoon but he was beginning to grow tired, till he was shaken awake when he saw another rider on the road. He had seen nobody till then. They were wearing a cloak and their face was hidden. He believed that they were a bandit to begin with. As the rider came by, he halted them. "I'll allow no bandit passage into the Grayewoods, I'm afraid. This area is already plagued enough, especially with the army mobilised and the Queen at Torem Coast."

"The Queen at Torem Coast? Thank you, traveller. I am to visit and speak with her about the coming invasion." the voice was female and Eric was initially shocked.

"It is strange then, that we now have the same destination." Eric's voice only barely pierced through the sudden gust of wind.

"You head to that dangerous place also? Why are two, both obviously not connected with the army, headed to a place where there is to be a vicious battle?" the other rider replied.

"If you ask why, I am afraid I cannot tell you. I am not sure if you are to be trusted. No offence, of course - my reason is complicated and important, and perhaps shall impact the fate of the whole South. Unless, of course, it is too late." Eric spoke once again.

"Can it be 'too late'? Is this thing that could be prevented so dreadful?" The woman asked.

"Indeed, Indeed!! A terrible fate could be drawn forth!"

"And what is your name, bearer of responsibility?"

"My name is Eric, and I am no more important than a servant of Castle Wormwood. And yours?"

She pulled down her hood, revealing long, blond hair and a pretty face.

"You may call me Ella."

"If you wish to travel with me, Ella, than you may. And a fair warning I give if you do travel alone: These roads are plagued by bandits and they may attack at any time. If gold you have, gold you will give - these bandits will take everything they can muster from anybody they can find."

"And you are saying you can 'escort me'?"

"I've been known to shoot an arrow or two." It was the first time she noticed the quiver full of arrows and the bow on his back.

"Then, let us ride, Eric."

*   *   *

A thunderous smash sounded in the dark forge. The sweaty, gray-skinned gnome's brown beard glinted in the light of the slowly bubbling lava. The hammer struck again, thus sharpening the glimmering sword further. A few more of the slow but echoing, heavy strikes gave its serrated, razor edge a sharp, dangerous glint. The sword was made of a dark, cobalt metal known by Gnomes as Adamant Steel. Brassy-red runes resembling the colour of dragon's blood had been embossed on its blade. The gnome began to proclaim loudly , which could be clearly heard, even over the bubbling of lava:

"Eht emoc si sah emit! Awak eysgal! Emit sah si emoc eht!" He thrust the sword up above his head, carrying it by its mahogany hilt which ended in a finely-cut ruby. Then, there was silence. The lava seemed to stop bubbling and no sound could be heard.

"I pronounce the great sword Dragontongue, the runic reaper, forged!!" The gnome placed the sword reverently upon a mantelpiece designed to hold such a weapon, wiped the sweat off his brow, then left the forge.

CHAPTER FIVE

BLOOD RETRIBUTION

The wagon cart's wheel creaked repeatedly. The only sound of the horse was the gentle hoofbeats that echoed quietly from the ground. The wind rustled through the newly grown spring leaves of the trees. All but for the sounds of nature the scene was silent. There was a crudely made wooden cage as the load of the wagon, and inside the cage was a man. It was odd for Vorodin to be silent, as the mad ex-King of Starbill was more often than not screaming. It seemed he was taking no action on his imprisonment; if he did, however, the rider would have been certain to die in the explosion. The prisoner was motionless as well. He was not dead - the rider had prodded him with a stick a few minutes before - and felt that he was breathing. Barely.

The King's time seemed short.

*   *   *

The crown quivered on King Isaak's unworthy head. He had placed it on his skull only hours before, refused the waste of time of a coronation, and almost immediately had the army of Starbill marching to Torem Coast. The two locations of Vlendale and Torem Coast were only a week's march away from each other, and Isaak was glad for the fact - he could hardly wait to see King Henry's face rammed upon a wooden stake and his body left to the crows. He was certain that in such a time of change the King would be weak, he would be disorganised and disorientated when an army from Starbill came to step on his toes. He was even more certain that they would not see the invasion coming; all spies were being concentrated in the North. Isaak was also sure that any traitors amongst his army would be discovered. Still, as he rode on his furry, white, agile mare Silkback, a twinge of nervousness bit at his confidence. As the army marched, they encountered nothing, it seemed all evaded their path, and all had abandoned the roads which had been held up by bandits, who had long since cleared the area of their setup and fled into the woods. Isaak was glad to herd them into the Grayewoods, for when Henry returned (if he lived past the battles of Torem Coast) he would be forced to clear the grounds of his castle of the pesky bandits. He looked backwards at the horde behind him. An admirable amount of soldiers. Most were young, and many would die. Some had been unwillingly conscripted. But all Isaak saw was a large army ready for combat. He did indeed not notice those who were frightened and scared, and if he had, he would have had no compassion for them.

*   *   *

"The savage man Duke Henry has taken over? Alas, it is as the Orb told. The Tyrans shall come and they shall kill us all."

"Go to your inner peace, Brother Dak. These are trivial matters. Our Dynasty shall remain safe in these southern mountains. It has been Foreseen." another monk named Father Dain said.

"Ay, brother. Peace. But it shall not stay this way, for all that is Foreseen is not definitive." a third man joined the conversation.

"But alas, Father, alas, Brother, the Orb showed us two possibilities: the one you speak of requires our own action: and that we are incapable of. But the other possibility shall result in death everywhere. Including in this hall! Grim times are ahead."

"Dak, the Orb only shows the *likely* possibilities. Many others may come and we shall be fit to stay here. We can allow those who have true power to truly act upon this. And if they may choose for all of us to perish, than so be it. Peace shall become true always, even after periods of great war." Father Dain's wisdom was appreciated by all but the roguish Brother Dak, who after hearing all the wisdom of many monks was still unsatisfied with the prospect of inaction. He spoke,

"Brothers, it would be a pilgrimage to leave these mountains and take action. Our wisdom should be useful against spiritual enemies - not that the Tyrans are without bodies in any sense. They are perhaps the most well-bodied human-like creatures in our realm." Dak was still in refusal.

"And if you do think that a pilgrimage of this type would be the answer to the best possible Peace, then go on the pilgrimage you must, Dak. All monks of the Dynasty work to find the best Peace, and if you truly think Peace can be found in helping War, then you must go." the third monk's name was Brother Dai-No-Kai, and his wisdom was perhaps the most unconventional of all the monks of the Dynasty.

"Brothers, if it is only I that see the use of this pilgrimage, then alone I shall go. But determined and unstoppable I shall be." Dak's voice did not falter.

"Brother Dak. I can only advise that you be careful. Take the Cross that bounds you to the Dynasty and take your bamboo staff too; without protection you cannot be." Dain chose his words cautiously.

"Aye, and what better protection than a fellow monk on your pilgrimage? I shall join you, Brother Dak." Brother Dai-No-Kai seemed eager to leave the mountain.

"Brothers, I looked in upon the room of the Orb this early morn. And what I saw was truly disturbing. You have a great chance of bringing Peace, but beware this: the tunnels that make the exit of this mountain have been unused for a long time, and… be careful. There are more than a few ways death could find you in that horrible, dusty, musty maze."

*   *   *

The sword strike was only barely deflected by the disgruntled Thomas. Henry had made seven strikes already and had left no opportunity for Thomas to attack back. Louis had tried to charge Henry, but the King had stepped aside and Louis had simply shattered his face into the mirror, thus making him fall to the ground, out cold. However, Thomas' blood was slowly boiling into strength and dexterity, lending him advantages over the slightly stiff older man. As Thomas fell into his fighting routine, he darted in a few attacks. They all missed, but Henry quickly realised that the soldier he was facing had talent. Henry's sword once again collided with Thomas', but instead of simply deflecting the hit, Thomas decided to push his sword down upon Henry. The strength of Thomas pushed the King to the ground. The man was only barely keeping Thomas at bay. But as Henry's sword was almost swung into his own neck, three knights rushed into the room, and all of them pointed their swords at Thomas. Thomas looked briefly at them, but it was opportunity enough for Henry to push him off and kick him in the stomach, making the soldier who had been so talented moments before lapse to the ground, winded. Then, he was punched by one of the knights, knocking him straight out. Henry was standing in milliseconds, retaking his look of formality and sturdiness. "In six days, men, we shall publicly execute them in front of the whole army. With guillotines. We shall put their heads on the first stakes the Tyrans see and yes, afterwards their headless bodies can be thrown in the ocean. Good night, fellows." one of the knights asked if Henry had suffered any injuries, but the King blew the comment aside and told them to simply get the three men chained up, have squires ride to Rosewick to fetch three guillotines, return and then sharpen them.

*   *   *

The two travellers had made camp quickly and had had an uneventful eve. Eric had found a few birds for them to eat, but Ella had seemed somewhat unadjusted to the meaty taste of game, in the same way she seemed unadjusted to waking up early the next day. Of course, by midday they were riding full speed. They scarcely encountered anybody that morning, just a single farmer headed to Castle Wormwood to sell his crops. He had seemed troubled and had given them little more than a nervous nod till he said:

"Be good 'n' careful on dose roads ahead of yeh. Bandits a robbed me of all the gold I had in my pockets."

After the farmer had been long gone, Eric spoke slowly and quietly:

"We could avoid them easily in these trees. But then, they would continue to plague these roads. We could clear them out."

"Clear out a group of bandits? Sounds dangerous and something two lone travellers are incapable of." Ella responded.

"Fine," Eric accepted, "But if we are attacked, they shall have advantage. And that is something I am wary of."

not much time later, the two travellers were nearing the edge of the forest when they saw the first signs of bandits. Eric spotted horse tracks along the same path they were riding upon, then they heard conversation up ahead. Eric held his finger to his lips at Ella, then turned to stealthily crawl to a viewpoint. He could see a campfire and a few men around it. Above the campfire was meat, cooking slowly. All three bandits were talking.

"Now, I heard three scallywags who were rising up against King Henry were caught, and are gonna be executed publicly at Torem Coast in a week! Till' then, they'll be tortured, I assume."

"King Henry? I didn't know there was a new man on th' throne!"

71

"Aye, mate! Henry held a coup! And he has a great deal o' support, as well! Ousted Arora from her throne, 'e did! An' he's leavin' the bloody ex-Queen alive! Bad move, personally! Gives her and her supporters opportunities!"

"Like bloody' what, yer half-dead Magithan donkey?"

"Well, mate, I have had a few bastardingly good ideas for that Arora, I have! First, she could send messages to her friend, Princess Elaina - I 'eard she already bloody did - proves it's a bloody good idea - an' get help from 'er and Prince Isaak - or she could raise followers amongst the bloody army! She already had bloody three!!"

"Yer a ragin' alcoholic, yer fat asshole. Yer talkin bloody bloody' trash."

"Maybe I did, but ah speak bloody better than you, you bastard!!" An arrow flung itself into the bandit's head. The two others turned suddenly to Eric, who had gotten the surprise on them.

"Who -" The bandit was interrupted as an arrow flew into his heart. The last, who was the quietest, stood, and ran away - till another arrow pursued him and took him in the back of the neck. The clearing was then quiet save for the crackling of the campfire.

"So, you definitely have used a bow before, Eric." said Ella.

"It is incredible, Father, to know you have now crafted your masterpiece. This sword - Dragontongue, you named it - has been in the making for a year. May I see it?" The son of Durbain, the legendary gnomish forge master, was amazed that the sword his father had been speaking of for a year was finally finished.

"Aye, son. 'Tis a maddeningly sharp and fine blade, eh?" The gnome wearing a thick brown (greying) beard unwrapped the sword he had been holding in two hands, and laid it down upon the table.

"Father, you have outdone yourself."

"Bah! I could've made it better. It's not perfect - but it is natural, powerful and magical, just like a dragon."

"I have never seen such a fine blade. The King-smith could not have made one better."

"Hah, son, you have always been a flatterer. Nay, the King-smith was my teacher! He did not tell me all he knew. But then again, I have learnt much more since he died. But, on more important matters, this sword I made to be a defence against the Tyrans. But I have not yet told you this: two more masterful smiths have been

73

working with me on this, and we believe you shall be amazed. Do you remember Buergat? Or Terrgon?"

"Aye, father…. Buergat and Terrgon I do both remember."

"Well, they stopped by recently to hand me what they had made, and now the suit of armour and the sword are all finished. They were on their way to travelling to our main group of tunnels further West of here, as they believe that strength comes in numbers."

"Father, get on with it."

"Of course, my boy. Dragontongue comes with a matching set of armour. Both are magical and are perfect in my eyes. But we must find a warrior worthy of these legendary items!" Perhaps one who has the favour of draconic creatures, as Dragontongue draws strength from the eternal power of dragonfire and the Sun."

"But who? Who would have met dragons and not have helped killed the dragon or been slain? There has never been a friendship between Dragon and Man."

"Ah yes, my son. But I am a ponderer of great knowledge. Dragons do stop growing indeed, but humans have been too dense to notice. Once dragons have age equal to two thousand years and they are about the size of a small island, they stop! An incredible fact, eh? The mistake that it was thought that dragons left unchecked are unstoppable has been their one trait that humans have been afraid of! If they would listen, Dragons could be the answer against the Tyrans!!"

"Yes, but to befriend dragons…"

"Son. You are persistent, aren't you. The name Baledor truly does suit you. It means 'stubborn' in ancient Gnomish. But you already knew that."

"Father, you take every chance to bring that up, I swear." Both of them began laughing.

*　　　*　　　*

The two men had begun their journey down into the catacombs only hours before, and were already struggling in the musty tunnels. "Will this never end? Almighty Lord, give us light!" Brother Dai-No-Kai was beginning to regret his choosing to accompany Brother Dak. The other monk was still pressing on through the tunnels and had seemed to only relish the cave air.

"Brother Dak, it must be time to rest now."

"Nay! Remember Father's warning: we must be careful in this labyrinth. If we were to rest, surely a terrible fate shall befall us."

"Then we can take turns watching! It will be easy."

Dak made a choking sound. "Like you'd ever not rest while you had the chance."

"Pay respect to fellow Brothers, Dak. You have always been watched carefully by the Fathers."

"What about you, Kai? You have killed many souls and all your sins have not yet been purged. You, too are unconventional."

"Why, then. We should be bad representatives of the Dynasty in northern Rosewick." Kai's response was unfalteringly true.

"Now you hath made us both out of comforts. 'Tis not a monk's position to do such a thing. The Almighty Lord scorns you." Dak was wearing a scornful grimace.

"This, alas, is unhelpful. Two battling monks cannot go on pilgrimage together! What terrible companions we are!"

"Maybe, but -" The rocks beneath them began to collapse into the ground, making way to a net, and below the net metal spikes. They thudded down into the net and a shape appeared above them.

"Two humans, unharmed and unarmed!"

*   *   *

The wagon had gone through the town silently. There had been a cage in the back of it, covered in a cloth so the citizens of Yinberg could not see what was within. Any that reached up to the cloth were given a strange look from the driver of the wagon, who all noticed was armed. It had passed through quickly but not quietly - only minutes after it had first arrived rumours were spreading all around about what sort of creature could possibly be contained inside. The cage was later unloaded onto a ship headed to Magyther. The driver had not accompanied the sloop, which was often known as 'the Ferry'. The Ferry took mad and dying Wraith-Touched people who could not be coped with all the way to the place where they were all held. Business was good for the ferryman - the channel between the kingdoms of Rosewick and Starbill (which were unseparated by water) and Magyther was relatively short and there were islands in-between making easy stops - the journey only took just over two days. All knew Magyther was bigger than both other Southern kingdoms, but it had the least might. It was almost entirely under the control of strange religious orders and occult guilds. The Ferry had left later that

afternoon, and the town soon forgot about the strange
wagon and what may have been transporting.

*   *   *

The army of Rosewick had reached Torem Coast and
had erected a large war-camp.

"You're saying what now, young squire? An army from
Starbill comes to lay waste to us? Are they criminally
insane? Now the entire South shall have even less chance
of surviving the Tyran attack! Oh, now I remember.
Isaak took the throne for himself. Perhaps the young man
discovered I had made it to the throne. That indeed is
almost certainly why he has made this risky move. Make
preparations, Voss. Have the soldiers build defences out
of the trees that will get in the way! Have them drill
harder than ever before! There can be no time wasted
for this: we need to be as prepared as possible! Young
squire, t'was you who discovered this, no?"

"Yes, your royal majesty. And I have told no others." said
the squire as Henry drew his sword.

"Kneel, young one." The squire went down on one knee
in front of his King. Henry brought the sword down to
the squire's shoulder.

"I am honoured, your majesty." said the squire. Henry then turned the blade so its sharp end faced the squire's neck. He then decapitated the squire, ripping the sword through the gangly neck of the teen. As crimson blood sprayed all over the war council tent, Henry hissed, "None other than those in this room and the greatest Knights of our ranks may hear of this news. No soldiers or squires are permitted to know."

"Your majesty, none shall discover. This battle shall be held a secret till it happens."

"Good. We do not need deserters now. If they were to discover they were to be in two battles, then I'm sure that more than a few of the cowards will slink away."

"Aye, your majesty. Your wisdom may have just saved lives."

CHAPTER SIX

HATRED OF ANCIENT SOULS

Eric and Ella stood dormant in the clearing. "Arora is no longer Queen, then." said Ella, breaking the silence.

"It is my fault! We should have gone quicker!!" Eric's outburst was sudden.

"How indeed is it your fault, Eric? I see no way you have empowered Duke Henry."

"I knew of the coup and was riding to tell Arora. But now it is obvious I am too late. Far too late to take any action against Henry - but perhaps not too late to help Arora escape."

"Duke Henry is king? I heard not when they said the name of that foul man." Responded Ella.

"Aye, Henry. Do you know of him?"

"Yes! I am of the lands of Starbill; perhaps you are familiar with the fact that James II, Duke Gallance of Halcore and Duke Henry of Norlick waged war upon us in their primes!? We as a country only barely survived."

"Then he is too a war criminal - moreover, I am sure Gallance and he sent people to kill me."

"Because you knew of their plan?" Asked Ella.

"Indeed. But I killed all of the soldiers they sent."

"Good then, for I would expect them to come after us again if they still lived."

*　　　*　　　*

Brother Dak and Brother Dai-No-Kai awoke in near-darkness. There were only two sources of light in the room, and each torch was being held in the hand of Gnome. The half-sized men were both stony-faced. Both were dressed in battered and stained leather armour. One only had stubble decorating his chin, and the other had a full-grown scruffy beard seemingly stamped onto his neck. Both of their demeanours seemed forced. Dak and Kai were both held in chains separately in chairs. Before they could even speak, they could hear talking and footsteps from the one exit from the room.

"Now, why must I attend to these prisoners? There is much polishing to do of the weapons I have made, and the wielder of the newly-forged Dragontongue is yet to be found." A fatter Gnome wearing the garments of a smith entered the room. "You insolent creatures, why have ye imprisoned two bloody monks of the Dynasty!?" The new gnome smashed the two monks' chains with a hammer he had been holding, and both were immediately free. "Our race truly does respect your religion, it does - please allow us to sincerely apologise for this rough treatment."

"This foul treatment is an insult! The Lord scorns you for this terrible treatment of his messengers! Away, away foul things! I shall have no such criminals touch my blessed skin. You and your own Gods be cursed and have a bad fate! Ay me! I just remembered your religion. There is no true God of the Forge. The one you speak of is a false idol! May he kiss the smooth buttocks of the Devil, for he is a pretender. And the God of the Mines. Ay me! How could a God be interested in dark tunnels where foul creatures crawl! No such God that was not a pathetic pretender could ever be such a one. And the God of the Caves! What be the difference between the sprawling caverns and winding mines? Your system is born of falsehood. Goodbye and good day, criminal!" Dak's speech reverberated through the caves.

"You are quite right, Brother. In fact, I do not worship any gods in any sense. I do not believe in Gnomish Gods or your one God either." replied the Gnome who had freed them.

"Goodness! Such a horrible disbeliever!" Dak took the amulet from his neck and raised it above Durbain's head. "Find your faith in the Lord, the one true deity." As Kai always did, he sighed.

"Friend Gnome, it makes me joyful to see such respect for the men of the Dynasty in a foreign civilisation with foreign deities. If you could simply direct us out of the mountains, then we shall be on our way, and get out of yours." intervened Dai-No-Kai before Dak could verbally assault the Gnome any further.

"Ah, a clever speaker! My name is Durbain, and I have a favour that I would ask of you. You seem perfectly suited for this task. If you refuse, I shall hold nothing against you."

"If we can repay you in any way if you help us, we must."

"Good! I like enthusiastic workers. Your task is a journey, one that will take you far. And this journey, I believe, will take you where you were already headed. You must head up North to the higher sectors of Rosewick and Starbill and find one worthy of the great sword Dragontongue and its paired armour. The armour and sword altogether are not heavy, and are easily carried. They were finely forged. I digress. The one you find must be perfect for saving this southern realm and if possible must have had a meeting with a Drake or Dragon and survived without slaying the beast or causing it any harm. The quest is great and I do not often ask strangers such things, but I feel it was meant to be. You are of the Dynasty, and I trust your judge of character. Be swift, but do not leave immediately -

there is a feast tonight - and there is no Gnomish feast that would you could possibly want to miss."

"Good Durbain, we are obliged to accept your task. And we too now know for sure that this is fate, and a responsibility has been laid on our shoulders. We accept." Kai said this after a glance at Dak's face which was beginning to take on a prideful smile.

*   *   *

"We're to be executed with a guillotine like other great achievers? Wahoo!! This is fantastic, what a merry fate awaits us! You know, some of the nicest guys I know are headless." Louis was beginning to go mad with expectancy.

"Hey, Louis. It won't be for a few days yet. I'll expect somebody will come and save us just as we're lined up to be killed. Like in a fairytale. And it'll be Eric who saves us! And we'll be like, 'Yay! We're saved!' But then we'll be skewered to the ground by arrows, and we'll be like, 'It was fun while it lasted'."

"You too, Edward? Wow, I guess neither of you can cope with the facts. We're going to die. Publicly." Thomas ended the conversation with the unpleasant facts, and the three men did not talk again till the next day.

*   *   *

"Your majesty King Isaak, Torem Coast is only two days' march away from us now. But there has been an... issue." The scout by the side of the cold-hearted King seemed to shrink down.

"What issue, Jack?"

"My name is Jake, your majesty -"

"I care not for the names of scouts. Tell me now, Jack." Isaak's impatience was becoming obvious.

"I believe they've noticed us, your majesty. They have started building defences where we'll strike them. It is as if they have looked straight into our war plans."

"Leave me, pathetic one. This is a matter that must be discussed."

"Yes, your majesty."

Isaak called his most trusted advisors forward, and began to speak with them. "You are clever ones, my advisors: we need a strategy. Henry has seen us coming, and is building defences. He'll cower behind them till he finds some advantage, then come out and rip us to shreds. It is his defending tactic. But this time he has only half a dozen days to prepare."

"Your majesty, perhaps we should wait until the Tyrans come. If the invaders are defeated, Henry will be weak and his army torn. And if he were to be defeated, then we would be able to outrun the Tyrans and get back to our castle. Then we have Henry and Rosewick as a shield."

Isaak half-hissed half-whispered once again: "A shield that will be destroyed. The Tyrans shall shred them with shear numbers, size and strength. Those barbarians can each take three good soldiers. Henry is hopeless, if I have it all worked out, unless he has some plan or manoeuvre to escape. But I cannot let him be killed by those simple brutes. I want to kill him myself. For all the people of Starbill he killed."

"Your wish should be granted, my King. And I may have a solution. In order to conduct my plan, however, we shall need far more troops. You are familiar with the river that runs out to the sea near here, correct?"

"Yes, Baron?"

"We take ships out via there, where we are too far away to be noticed but near enough to take action. All our troops are spread out across some ships. We take the ships to the end of land, but then we wait. When the Tyrans arrive, we sail out, hopefully with the wind billowing in our favour, and we will spearhead into their backsides. Because the Tyrans will be fighting a war on two fronts, they'll be defeated. Because we came from behind and most would be concentrating on the battle in front, Henry's army would have suffered much greater losses, thus rendering us a victor against the Tyrans and Rosewick, and perhaps conquering us this entire continent."

"Baron, your plan is fantastic, and will not be expected! Henry will not see it coming."

"Exactly, your majesty."

"But there is indeed one small problem. Where do we claim more troops from?"

"Your majesty, are you familiar with the Mercenary's Guild situated in the forest between Starbill and Rosewick near the Southern mountains?"

"Indeed. It would be unfortunate, however, to need the help of pathetic creatures such as those paid warriors."

"Ah, but your majesty, even they would not benefit if the Tyrans came here. It's a mutual interest between the Guild and us."

"You're right. Send word to the Mercenary's Guild and have the entire guild hired. We'll pay them half of their usual salary as this helps them as much as it helps us. An excellent plan you have made, Baron. I applaud you."

*   *   *

The defences were going well. Henry had observed Voss pushing his soldiers to work hard, and hard did the soldiers work. Henry really found himself admiring the man's ability to push strength out of the men. They were all adept at the simple, labouring tasks of lugging wood around and hammering planks into place. Others were more skilful, and were placed as overseers over the others. The ones who couldn't cope with the lifting were either assigned to hacking away at the trees themselves or were simply forced to patrol and scout the area alongside the squires. Those who fell to doing that often fell further down in the ranks of popularity among the soldiers. Of course, the defences themselves were being designed by Battlemaster Voss as well. Henry wasn't entirely sure of the intelligence (if any) in the man's brain, but he could get the soldiers to do anything, and it came naturally that the responsibility of designing the defences came to him as well.

*   *   *

Eric and Ella made their way along the road slowly. The bandits they had encountered that morning had unwillingly told them exactly what they needed to know. They had decided not much earlier before that they would still make their way to Torem Coast and instead help Arora escape from her captivity. It wouldn't be easy, they both knew that. Both were thinking as their horses trotted slowly, and there was silence save the minor din of the horses trotting and birds singing in the trees, till they came to a point where the road ended. "The road isn't supposed to end here." the road had abruptly stopped, and forest had begun.

"Yes," Said Ella, "It is supposed to cut through here. Strange."

"Unless we have somehow made a wrong turn? Actually, scratch that. Let's go through the forest ourselves. I've always loved the woods and I know how to deal with all such creatures to be found in groves in this area."

"As long as we don't go on foot I'm willing to continue, as long as you can guarantee this will be safe? What if we encounter the rest of the bandits those three belonged to?"

"Bandits rarely form groups larger than half a dozen. If we encounter any, I think we should be fine!"

"Then, good Eric, let us go." They entered the woods at a faster pace than they had been at before.

Five minutes later, after a potent smell of rotten meat had reached the noses of both the travellers, Eric spoke.

"There is something following us. The rustling bushes? Not the wind."

"I have noticed it too. Something large is nearby."

"Sss…. Intrudersss…" they turned to a large shape behind them. A large, lizard-like creature was before them, and it looked aggressive. "Thisss… isss… my… territory… Sss…"

Drakes and dragons were known for their ability to communicate, and the chilling, slithery voice struck Eric to the very bone.

"We are here for no fight, beast." Eric was the first to speak of the two travellers.

"Why, then, do you intrude? Ssss…"

"We are passing by."

"None… Ssss… Come by without making themssselvess worthwhile to me…"

"Then what do you seek? Gold? Food? Both I can supply at least a little of." Eric's nervousness was beginning to slip away.

"No… A ssservice you could do…" the drake's tongue lolled around in its mouth momentarily.

"Deep in the foressst wasss once my territory… Decadesss ago… Sssss, but then they came. They pushed me out of my home. Ssso now, I am here. And thossse oness are dangerousss, the oness that took my home…"

"If you will give us safe passage," Eric glanced at Ella, "We accept."

"Sssafe passsage can be guaranteed, humansss. But thisss favour iss not ssafe at all…"

"Then lead us there. It should be quick work."

"Sss… You are too confident for your own… Ssss… good." The large red drake turned away and began running deeper into the forest. Eric and Ella easily sped alongside the beast on their horses.

$$*\qquad*\qquad*$$

"And here is Dragontongue itself. A fine sword, eh?" Durbain had just shown Brother Dak and Brother Dai-No-Kai the set of armour and was showing them the great sword. As Kai marvelled at how light but also huge and sharp it was, Dak engrossed himself in the network of intrinsic brassy runes all over the sword. Both were amazed by how stunning the weapon was. The armour had been similar: made of dark, blue-tinged metal and bulky but not heavy at all. The armour, too had had red, deep-cut runes in it and Kai had felt the need to wear the armour and wield the sword. The warrior inside him was stirring.

It was getting to the evening when they were invited to the Ceremony of Stone. There was such a ceremony every week, and supposedly the ritual kept away 'bad spirits' which used to plague the tunnels. Many Gnomes wearing robes were standing in a circle in the middle of the large room. A circle of large stones balanced on top of each other building all up to the ceiling was around them.The rest of the people who lived in the Gnomish settlement were standing all around them. All the robed Gnomes began chanting, and Dak whispered to a Gnome next to him "What is this about?"

"It is a religious tradition praising the God of Mines and the God of Caves and asking them to keep the Wraiths out of our tunnels."

"Ay me!! STOP!!!! SUCH AN ACT AGAINST THE LORD WILL MAKE HIM ANGRY, AND HE SHALL SMITE THIS ENTIRE MOUNTAIN!!! STOP IF YOU LOVE YOUR LIVES!!! STOP IF YOU LOVE THE LORD!!!" the shout pierced through the chanting.

"YOU IDIOT!!! NOW WRAITHS SHALL COME!!!!" the Gnome next to Dak exploded in fury. The stones arcing up to the ceiling began to tilt and rumble.

"It's happening." said a Gnome nearby. Suddenly a Gnome ran up to Dak and Dai-No-Kai and handed them Dragontongue and its corresponding armour.

"Run now. Be swift and leave the mountain before sunset, when they'll become strongest. Run I told you, run like the wind!! And remember Durbain, and me, his son, Baledor!! Remember who forged these!!"

Dak began to run, but Dai-No-Kai grabbed him and shouted in his face.

"What have you done!? These Gnomes who have shown us hospitality have been doomed by you, you insolent scum!"

As three ghostly shapes appeared in the circle, the stones cracked and fell to the ground, smashing and squishing many Gnomes. The few of the robed Gnomes that did survive began to scream with pain as a ghostly hand appeared beneath each of them and lifted them off the ground, then squeezed the small being with two fingers till the body lost feeling and became deadweight, and the soul inside was devoured. The hands began to multiply. Dai-No-Kai and Dak looked at each other briefly, then ran. They stumbled through the tunnels and as it grew darker and darker, they knew the sun was beginning to dip its head below the earth. They rushed down into the uninhabited catacombs and as screams and shouts echoed down to them, they took no notice and continued running. Once or twice they saw the ghostly apparition of a Wraith, but they escaped far before they could even be spotted by the wrathful spirit. They found the one exit of the mountain, and discovered it to be closing. A larger wraith-hand was pushing a rock in front of the exit. Dak held up his cross, and said:

"The Lord scorns thee, unholy spirit!!" The hand was almost unaffected by the prayer, but seemed to weaken ever so slightly. As a hand appeared behind them, Dai-No-Kai whipped out the one weapon he had on himself: Dragontongue. He attempted to keep the spirit-hand away by slicing at it. The weapon somehow cut straight through the normally impervious hand, and destroyed it.

"This sword truly is a masterpiece."

Dai-No-Kai, suddenly empowered with strength, kicked the rock closing down upon the exit, made it roll down the hill below, and sliced the hand that was pushing it. He quickly put the sword back in the scabbard he had been given and he and Dak rushed down to the bottom of the hill, where no hands seemed to appear. Still, they continued running till they had disappeared far down into the forest. It was not till an hour later that they finally felt safe once again. "Dak, you have wronged this world again."

"I could not help it, brother. It was against the code of the Dynasty!! We could not allow blasphemy! It was a ritual to the God of the Mines and the God of the Caves! You should have helped me put a stop to it."

"Yes, but do you realise that the ritual must usually work? The fact that it failed one time made such a difference? 'Tis proof that the Gnomish Gods do too exist. And so does our Lord. It is the great Belief that grants the air power. In our own way, we empower the Lord to help us, by giving him Belief. In the same way that the Gnomes empower their Gods by giving them Belief. 'Tis Belief and prayer that gives Gods power. For if none of us believed in the Lord, he would not help any of us - or hurt any of us. He affectively have no power, because he would have no reason to use it."

"Brother Dai-No-Kai, you have grown in wisdom. I can understand that point of view, you have explained it well - but I shall keep to my own ways. For now. If you attempt to preach me again, I shall allow you to. But I shall not necessarily take these beliefs to heart."

"Good, brother. You learnt a lesson. But over a hundred lives have been sacrificed for it."

"Over a hundred Lord-scorning lives."

"Give different Gods belief. Perhaps they shall take away your stubbornness."

"Ha. Never."

"This is a serious matter, Brother. You have killed many today. Perhaps your sins can be rewritten as good acts, however, if we save these Southern lands."

"Kai. We shall. We shall. 'Tis a pilgrimage."

Chapter Seven

FORT OF GREMLINS

Eric had barely set eyes upon the fortress built into the hills and the creatures around it before he felt the spurring of hatred in his blood. The fortress looked as if it had been built by bandits or outlaws, but they had clearly been long since overrun. "Sss… Timesss change. But thossse who live in thisss place are ssstill my enemies. Sss… Attack."

"Before we attack, what is your name?"

"Voklasss…."

Eric nocked an arrow into his bow, then paused. He only then realised the creatures before him were dreaded Goblins and Trolls. The Goblin curse was spread by the bite of a Troll or Goblin. Whereas Goblins could only infect small animals, Trolls could infect anything they could get their teeth upon.

"But these are Goblins! And Trolls! If any of us are bitten…"

"Sss… I am unafraid. Draconic creaturesss are immune…"

"They have no way to harm you then! Sure, the Trolls are big and strong and hardy, but you can take them. I think we are not needed."

"I am weaker than you think. Sss…" After the Drake had spoken, Eric counted the creatures he could see.

"There are not many of them. A dozen at most."

"And you… Sss… think there are no more in the fort itssself?"

"I see your point." Eric let his arrow fly. The projectile went straight into a Goblin's head, ending its life. Two more attacks quickly followed from his bow, both of the shots ending the life of another Goblin. Then, Voklas pounced out of the trees and ripped through the sinewy tendons of a Troll's shoulder, severing its right arm straight off and causing the bloody limb to fall to the ground. Ella drew a dagger from her belt, but stayed put in the bushes and trees alongside Eric, who continued to pelt arrows into the crowd of creatures. Voklas was killing many and once again Eric reasoned in his mind that the Drake could have managed the battle by itself, till about thirty more Goblins and around seven more Trolls came rampaging out of the doors of the wooden fortress.

*   *   *

"King Henry, one of our scout ships found the incoming Tyran fleet. It seems, in fact, that two fleets are coming. One coming here, the other slipping down Minnow River inland."

"Saint George!! What have we seen around the river lately?"

"I told you before, sire. We have seen the Starbill army building boats there."

"Hahaha!! Fate loves Rosewick. Starbill will be destroyed while we win against the other fleet! But, ahem, how big is the fleet that comes our way?"

"I would estimate that they will have more troops than us."

"Why, then. We shall need to forcefully enlist many more soldiers. And the size of the fleet going to attack Isaak?" King Henry had a worried expression on his face.

"Smaller, your majesty. But not too much smaller. I fear that the entire South shall fall."

"Damn it! We may as well have already bloody fallen."

"Agreed, your majesty. We may need to retreat to Castle Wormwood. This position is not the best one tactically." The king's advisor was known well for his cowardice.

"I will not cow back to our stronghold. We must be valiant! We must train our soldiers as much as we can, bring in more of them, have more catapults built and prepared. Even lining the way up here with traps! We must glean every advantage we can find."

"Yes, yes, your majesty. We shall find many more troops, prepare traps… We shall be ready for the invasion."

"Oh, and have spies focused on Isaak and his plans. We do not want any… surprises," said the King, "Oh, and have the guillotines yet arrived?"

"Yes. They are being polished and sharpened this day ready for tomorrow. The executions, I believe, will spur a sense of nationalism among our troops."

"Well, this long wait before the invasion is having my blood boiling. I want to hear screams. Let us torture them a little. Enjoy them while we have them."

"Of course, sire! But I shall remain here and wait for any news while you have your… fun."

*   *   *

"Brother, this is a good spot to rest." The clearing in the woods was not littered with twigs as the rest of it was, and a small mint plant was spreading its scent throughout the clearing.

Dai-No-Kai was beginning to lose his breath.

"Two minutes, brother. You are allowed two minutes."

"Others as well need to breathe, Dak. But two minutes shall suffice. With your young stamina still in you, I am not surprised you are still ready to run." Dai-No-Kai collapsed on the ground.

"Brother, do not fake death just to get another minute to get your breath back. It is unkind."

"And also unkind is killing a settlement of Gnomes, brother. You must find your peace and accept others for who they are. Then your sins will stop multiplying."

"Do not speak, brother. I thought you were trying to get your breath back."

"Dak, I am just laying on the ground now."

"Get up, you oaf. 'Be swift!' They told us. With all your 'deaths' we shall never arrive where we need to go! In fact, we do not even yet have a destination!"

Kai got up from the ground. "Fine. Let us 'Be swift!'."

"I appreciate that you comply, brother. We must be quick on this pilgrimage! Quick, quick, quick."

The two monks started walking through the forest once again. They passed by ponds, trees and rabbit burrows. They took no heed of the peaceful surroundings and simply travelled. "Kai, who are we looking for to wield these treasures?"

"We shall know, I think, when we find them."

"No, their demeanour."

"Well, I believe we are looking for one vigilant, intelligent and strong enough to be a hero without the sword, and one kind and wise enough to be one we would be proud to call a fellow monk."

"A monk cannot be a hero. We do not glorify ourselves. We could not call the one we were with a monk if they were a glorious hero."

"A point you have made, Dak." Suddenly, an arrow flew from the trees, thudding into the ground beneath Dai-No-Kai's feet. A large man walked out of the trees. "Welcome, gentlemen, to the forest."

"Who are you?"

"I bring no battle to messengers of the Dynasty. I am of the Mercenary's Guild, and can offer you a place to stay overnight and food. And if there may be any service we can do for you, then do it we shall - for the right price, of course."

"We do accept your offer of shelter, and if you would accept our payment, we would buy some horses."

"Horses, eh? Plenty of 'em at the Outpost."

"Good! We shall need horses very much! And very useful they shall prove I'm sure!"

"Then come, good Monks, for the sun shall not stay up forever."

*　　*　　*

"I am unafraid of that bastard King Henry or of the Tyrans. No matter who we face, I shall remain vigilant.

Niurmuc, have we received word yet from the Mercenary's Guild?"

"Aye, your majesty. They said they would ally alongside us, for the right price."

"We can pay enough if we defeat Henry and the Tyrans. If their help is adequate enough, then we can pay them. Otherwise, no."

"Don't you think this is just a bit too uncertain, your majesty? As if we are giving all of our trust in chance?"

"It did at first, Niurmuc. It did at first. But it does no longer! I know that Fate shall give us fortune and favour." Isaak, the King of Starbill, had a maddened look spread across his face.

"Of course, your majesty. I trust your decisions."

"My hunger for blood grows. Have some of the soldiers bring that horridly disfigured prisoner over." Niurmuc called, and minutes later a large shape was brought before the King, resembling Sir Rusga.

"You are a dead man, Rusga. A favourite toy of that awful Duke Gallance. You shall pay for his actions and your own, now." Isaak drew his sword from the scabbard by his side, and held it to the large man's neck. "When we found you, you had an arrow in your eye and your body had trample marks from a horse. Fittingly humiliating for the champion of Halcore." Isaak gently poked the end of his sword onto Sir Rusga's Adam's apple. "Die, you bastard." Isaak thrust the sword through the neck of the captive, the end of his blade coming straight through the other side. As Isaak's bloodlust cooled, so did Rusga's heart, and thus did the knight of Halcore die.

"Ah, it feels good to end the life of an enemy. Such satisfaction can never be found elsewhere." suddenly, shouts threw around the camp.

"Your majesty, we've discovered a problem!"

"And what may this problem be?" shouted Niurmuc, who was shocked by the suddenness of the event.

"A fleet from the Tyranlands heads our way! It's separated off from the main fleet now, which is headed to Torem Coast. It seems they want to use this river as a landing zone!" shouted a squire.

"How far!?" bellowed Isaak.

"Lord shall weep for we shall all die. They shall be here in a week!"

"Then how did we spot them?"

"We didn't. Some of our spies at Torem Coast discovered a day ago, and now the news has reached us."

"And those mercenaries are coming, right Niurmuc?"

"Of course, your majesty! But this sudden rush is not good, for they shall not arrive for some time! More than a week!"

"Then we shall just have to hold our position till they arrive, I'm afraid. The history of Starbill shall not end this year!" Isaak was having a rush of energy. "And Henry, too, shall have his fleet of Tyrans arriving?"

"Indeed, sire. Allies must be gathered, and quickly."

*   *   *

The frenzy rushed through Eric. His knife had become an extension of his arm, and it was carving through the skulls of all it could find. Goblins were falling left and right. Trolls were bleeding everywhere, and the number of the feral beasts was constantly dropping. He and Voklas had slain almost half of all of the Goblins and Trolls when the frenzy had first come, and a beast-like rage had taken over Eric. Now, he could only count two Trolls and a dozen Goblins littering the battlefield. The last few Goblins and Trolls fell and finally Eric was forced to calm himself.

"You are indeed a great warrior, human… Sssafe passsage is granted."

"Thank you, o great Drake. We accept this honour."

"But first, humansss, a gift…" The drake threw a golden ring into the hands of Eric, then turned away.

"Thank you, o great Drake. We shall be on our way." Eric and Ella made their way from the clearing, whispering to each other. "Voklas could have done that himself."

"Agreed. Why oh why did he need us?"

"The Lord knows." Eric and Ella jumped onto their horses and began riding out of the forest, quickly leaving the clearing and all the killing that had occurred there behind. They rode swiftly till they came out on the other side of the road. They found that the remainder of that road was unplagued by bandits and unused by travellers, likely because none went through the forest. As they slowly came to a sign on the road, they discovered that a river was nearby. Eric turned his head to the direction of the sign, and he saw the construction of boats. "Ella, do you see down there!? It looks like the army of Starbill is building boats to go down that river!"

"Whatever they are doing, it cannot be for the benefit of us. Let's take a closer look." Ella began riding down the hill.

"Of course. But let us do it stealthily." said Eric. The two riders reached the riverside camp quickly but quietly.

"We do indeed have little time to prepare for the Tyrans coming this way, your majesty." said a rat-faced man near a figure that Eric and Ella both recognised as Isaak.

They heard Isaak shout;

"Of course, Niurmuc. Of course. But we already had these boats, and I am strongly unafraid of what they can do to us. As long as those mercenaries get here soon!"

"Eric, there is something you should know. My name is not Ella. I am Princess Elaina of Starbill."

"And you tell me now!? When we are meters away from the King of Starbill?"

"That isn't the King, that's Isaak, my brother."

"Yes. King Isaak. Your brother is the King." Eric was surprised the sister of the King did not know who was king.

"Then what happened to my father?"

"Well, the public information was that he died."

"He died!? My brother had some hand in his fate, I'm sure. Or, alas, he is just being held prisoner." Elaina was growing louder and angrier by the second.

"Elaina, we must sneak away. They could notice us any minute…"

They crept away from the bushes.

$$* \qquad * \qquad *$$

Arora wept. Her child would be born roughly upon the day of invasion, and she doubted things could get any worse. The three soldiers who had tried to take the crown back from Duke Henry were to be killed the next day, the number of her handmaidens was reducing daily, and she had not yet received a reply from Princess Elaina. Things were desolate in the camp for everybody. Henry was grimly contemplating battle plans, knowing the fate of all the southern kingdoms was sealed, Thomas, Edward and

Louis were recovering from being tortured, the knights and warriors who were part of the defensive force wished they too had struck against the King when the time was right, envious of the quick and ceremonious deaths that would come to his attackers. Even the squires knew bad fates awaited all in the camp.

*   *   *

"Brothers, welcome to the Mercenaries' Guild Outpost. Here, we can supply those horses you need, an overnight stay and a warm dinner. And if needed, a bodyguard on the road." The mercenary motioned to the huge, well-structured and thick-walled wooden cabin with a tower sprouting from the middle that lay ahead of them.

"Ah, yes. Dinner. A bed-mat. A roof. I welcome these things!"

"Do not get too enthusiastic about materialism, Brother Dai-No-Kai. It is unwise to sway from the Dynasty's guidance." Dak was still uncertain of the trustworthiness of the mercenaries.

"I know, I know, Dak. But it has been a time - three days, perhaps - since we slept in a warm place with a roof over our heads."

"Hmm... I get your meaning, Brother. However, these mercenaries fight for money. It means they are capable of extreme violence and are good at surviving it. If they do not steal our money and kill us in these woods and we are never heard of again, then I would be surprised. But I would still never come here again."

"Of course you would not. These woods are filled with wolves and bears and hostile creatures. We've been lucky so far."

"I meant because I do not trust them. And you should not, either."

"The Lord's seventy-eighth statement: all are worthy of trust. Not all are worthy of kindness."

"No. It was the other way round. When was the last time you studied the Tomes Of The Dynasty?"

"A decade it has been since I last explored those books."

"Eons! Eons it has been. Longer than a decade! More likely two! I first studied the books a decade and a half ago. You, I remember, have not studied them since my initiation with the Dynasty."

"You are still an inexperienced monk. Thus I still tell thee: it has only been a decade. A ten-year experienced monk would make such comments to another."

"You are a tough man, Kai. A stubborn, tough, unchangeable man. But we must enter this death-of-ours now." the two monks entered the large log settlement and the door closed behind them, slamming loudly. "Hey, guys! Look!! Found two monks!" the mercenary shouted. After a minute of waiting, the mercenary looked surprised. He opened the door at the end of the hallway. "Look!" he shouted again, "Oh… I think they may have left."

"Left? An entire guild of mercenaries? This is even fishier than I imagined." Dak began walking towards the exit.

"Can you not see, Brother? This man is surprised. There are supposed to be dozens more mercenaries here."

"Emotions can be faked."

"By a warrior who is obsessed with money and can hardly count to ten? Unlikely."

"My friends, I am sorry for the inconvenience," the mercenary began, "They all left to go to war alongside King Isaak of Starbill. Of course, I was left behind. But instead, I can supply you two with all you need and serve as a bodyguard for you on your journey. For the right price, of course."

"We do not need protection, however a rest and some food of sorts would be welcome. And perhaps, if any remain, some steeds."

"Food should be readily found in these halls. There should be a few spare mares. If you have no need of me this visit, then I shall abandon this place and attempt to catch up with my fellow guild members."

"Go, man, go! Catch up with your fellows quickly so that you may join them!" Dak's persuasive voice echoed through the hall. "I shall! I shall! I will grab my weapons, my belongings and a steed. Farewell, my good monks! Farewell!"

"You are not gone yet, mercenary. But farewell indeed."

Minutes later, the mercenary was fully equipped and was wearing a huge halberd on his back.

"I trust you as monks of the Dynasty to make sure ye don't burn down this here building. See you after the war, if any of us survive." the warrior rushed out of the door and leapt upon a large horse waiting for him outside.

"And remember: the Mercenary's Guild showed you hospitality!" he rode away quickly, leaving the two monks behind.

"And now, brother, we have this place to ourselves. We may stay here for more than one night. We may do whatever we wish!"

"So, you purposefully rid this place of that man? Dak, you are cunning and villainous."

"And we may choose what horses we take. It was a simple choice and I chose the right one."

"Ah, Dak. Never change. The Lord still loves you even with your sins."

"I have sinned, but I have sinned for the love of the Lord and for the protection of the greater good. I sin for the dominance of holiness and to expel devilry. Someday, I may have to expel myself. I am unafraid of what I may become, for I shall always have the strength to destroy myself."

Chapter Eight

THE CRIMSON ARCHER

"A speech, all, before the executions. I am proud to be the King of these lands. And I am glad that so few of you resisted this good change that has certainly brightened the future of Rosewick." Cheers, whoops and clapping flew around the camp. The tents had been moved and a wooden structure had been placed on the ground. The King and a few of his closest advisors stood on the structure, while three soldiers had been tied up underneath the blades of guillotines. Their screams were supposed to be heard, and nothing had been placed over their mouths. "I am glad you share my optimism for our kingdom -"

"And he's even more glad this specific morn, since he joggled two balls this morning." Thomas's wit was sharp even when a blade was above his head. Laughter burst out across the war-camp. King Henry turned to his interruptor, and kicked the man in the face three times, squishing the nose of Thomas into his head and causing his face to burst out bleeding. He turned back to the crowd.

*   *   *

"As I was saying, our kingdom is flourishing under my rule and in this circumstance. I know we shall survive this onslaught we shall have to face. We will get stronger. We shall not be permanently marked. We shall not be cut deeply. We shall not even lose this battle! We shall push them from this continent we call Torem, and they shall never return. They shall have nightmares of our fierceness. They shall scream when we cut their throats. We shall shout when victory comes to us. And yes, we shall weep when the dead are buried. But grief brings anger and anger grants strength, thus making us unstoppable. WE SHALL BE VICTORIOUS!!!"

"WE SHALL BE VICTORIOUS!!!!"

"WE SHALL BE VICTORIOUS!!!!"

"WE SHALL BE VICTORIOUS!!!!"

"YES!!!! AND WE SHALL NOT FEAR!!!!"

"AND WE SHALL NOT FEAR!!!!"

"AND WE SHALL NOT FEAR!!!!"

"AND WE SHALL NOT FEAR!!!!"

"And these traitors will die. But first, if you would wish to fetch yourself a drink, then you may do so. In a minute, we shall see these traitors' heads decorating the spikes that shall drive fear into the hearts of our enemies!!!!"

"Elaina, there lies the war-camp that Henry uses as his own. Of course, it belongs to Arora."

"Then we must be slow and quiet. We can take our time. Eric, what is the chance that Arora is now dead?"

"I would not know, Princess. For all I know, she is to be executed right now." After Eric spoke, suddenly echoes reached them. "AND WE SHALL NOT FEAR!!!!"

"Henry must be speaking to a crowd. Let us get a closer look to see what this event may be."

They rode closer, and saw a wooden structure in the centre of the war-camp and a large crowd around it.

"Oh, god."

"What is it, Eric?"

"Those three pinned under guillotines? My three friends. They must have attacked that awful man as soon as he became king. Very much the behaviour I'd expect of Edward, Louis and Thomas."

"If they are warriors who would help us, then I'm sure it would be in our interest to save them."

"Yes, but how? There is a crowd of soldiers around them, most with weapons on their belts. Henry himself is dangerous, and his advisors too. But, if we rain arrows down upon that stage of death, then perhaps we shall force them to get away from my friends."

"Do you have a spare bow, Eric? Because the only weapon I hold is a dagger."

"Why would I ever carry more than one bow? It must be me to get my friends out of there. But, perhaps you can help, actually…"

"And how may that be?"

"You have a dagger. If you sneak behind the stage while I distract all of the soldiers and Henry and his advisors, then you cut their ropes so that they may escape."

"It sounds dangerous, but it may be the best plan we can formulate this quickly." Elaina quickly agreed to her role in the plan.

"Good! You sneak down there, I'll do what I need to do." The two riders separated. Eric rode forwards, straight towards the camp. He readied his bow and nocked an arrow from his quiver. He drew his bow as his horse flew down the hill, and then let fly. The arrow flew straight at its target, on a perfect trajectory till it pierced the skull of his first target.

The duke who had been Henry's most trusted advisor was now dead.

Screams and shouts started coming from the camp, and then they spotted the rider. Another arrow quickly followed, ending the life of another trusted advisor. The third advisor, sensing the trend, began running from the stage, till another missile caught up with him and took him through the leg. Eric then nocked two arrows. He drew back as he was used to doing, and let both arrows loose, both finding their target. Henry was lashed to the ground where he had been hit in his shirt and where blood came pouring out of an arrow wound in his forearm. He was alive, but pinned to the ground. The arrow had gone straight through his bones and had struck into the wooden stage underneath him. Meanwhile, soldiers from the crowd, mainly knights that were extremely loyal to King Henry, began charging at the lone rider. Infinitely outnumbered, Eric still found courage to ride on. Every arrow he fired found a home to embed itself in, most of them ending the life of their target. When a sword finally scratched Eric's horse, he knew the fight was about to become his death. He was thrown off and nearly trampled by his panicking horse.

He was a single man versus a hundred, but with the huge number of his attackers, most of their strikes ended up piercing and killing one of their own allies. Of course, Eric was torn to pieces till he had put away his bow and drawn his knife, and after slashing a few soldiers in hopeless conflict he dashed backwards out of the battle, head butting another man as he did so and disengaging. As he ran from the men in their clunky metal armour, he slowly got further and further away, till he managed to quickly vault onto his horse once more. His cloak was dyed red from all the blood that had tainted it. It was ripped and shredded, however the blood of Eric's own that was on the swords and knives of his enemies disturbed the huntsman more.

On the stage, he spied Thomas free, who had leapt upon the body of Henry and was strangling the pinned king to death. Soldiers began to snap out of their surprise and fear, and began to attack the three escaped prisoners as well as Elaina. She, Edward and Louis began to all run, but Thomas did not follow.

"Thomas!! You do not deserve death here and now!! Run!! I shall hold them off. Run!! If I can, I will kill them all and their damned king." Thomas looked briefly at Louis, then said:

"You are a brave man, Louis. I shall act according to your wishes." Thomas also ran, and Louis stayed behind. He picked up the dropped sword of the king of Rosewick.

"Come at me, bastards." said grim Louis as a horde of armoured men wielding swords and axes came roaring onwards towards him.

Edward, Thomas and Elaina leapt onto Elaina's horse which was only a few meters from the camp, and began riding away as fast as the horse could manage with three riders. They reunited with bloodied Eric on his horse minutes later. They only barely escaped from the camp, being followed temporarily by soldiers on foot.

As the bloodied people finally recovered from the battle, Edward switched horses to ride with Eric in order to preserve Elaina's horse's health.

"Saint George! We forgot Arora!!" said Eric suddenly, breaking the silence.

"We must go back for her!!" replied Elaina.

"We cannot now, and we all know it. They shall be on their guard now, and will specifically be guarding her and her tent. We have set off the alarm, thus we cannot save her."

"Louis sacrificed himself for us, so that we might have had a chance to escape. And a chance to return. Damn us! We are fools! But still, it would be dangerous transporting a pregnant lady on horse. I remember when she first said she was pregnant. It was a public announcement. I believe it has been nearly nine months since then."

"Then how did she mobilise the army and mobilise with it?"

"I believe they brought a chariot."

"Then we cannot do anything for Arora at this moment. She shall be trapped there till the baby is born, and it would have been cruel of us to take her with us."

"Agreed. Then we must wait till the time is right to strike again, and meanwhile be aware of Tyrans invading anywhere."

*　　*　　*

"The boats are ready?"

"All are made, your majesty. None have leaks and I fully expect that we shall surprise those Tyrans with our nautical ability. And, we of course know that the mercenaries are coming, and they shall arrive just after our battle begins."

"It is playing out well, is it not, Niurmuc. Things have gone well for you: you have gone from the Prince's advisor to the King's right hand." Isaak, although speaking to the man, was looking into the shallow water.

"Of course, your majesty. I have gone up in the esteem of our entire nation. I am a very trusted advisor. 'Tis a good life, that of a nobleman."

"You only came into this life recently. Before, I remember you plagued the streets of Vlendale with your damned gang, then I hired you because you are clever and you have sources of information."

"You knew I would do anything to rise in society. The way I became the leader of the gang was I killed the previous one. I was his most trusted second-in-command..." Isaak was completely oblivious to the threats that Niurmuc was slipping into his speech.

"... But he trusted me too much, and I got sick of him. He never listened to my ideas, he only trusted me to get the job done… But times have… changed and I am no longer part of a gang of thugs. But I am part of an army that is rivalled by other armies, in the same way gangs are rivalled by other gangs. Perhaps things shall go the same way."

"Yes, your gang rose above the others. I share your optimism! We shall - no - we must - come out on top."

"Not under your rule…" muttered Niurmuc to himself.

*   *   *

Dak and Dai-No-Kai had eaten a full dinner and had slept a good night's sleep, and in the morning they changed their minds about staying. They would continue on their journey immediately, as they both knew time was running out.

They left early in the morning and came out of the woods an hour later.

"It is good to be out of that gloomy forest. Now we can truly appreciate the sun."

"Aye. The sun. It only rose recently, and we still have time to travel far. Perhaps we can stop at Dusk Hill tonight for rest. Never has there been a more innocent farming village."

"Fine, Kai. We shall go to Dusk Hill. I know you lived there before the Magithan War ruined your life. I too, once lived in a village. But it was destroyed, if you remember rightly. Smashed into the ground by trolls and goblins. I shall never forgive the gremlin-like creatures that so displease the Lord."

"As the legend tells, you are right. They do so displease the Lord. 'Tis said he created them by accident when he was inexperienced. And he could not rid the world of them because the numbers of them increased so quickly. But he did remove a little of their power: he removed their ability to infect large creatures. However, the large creatures that were already infected kept the ability, thus separating Goblins and Trolls."

"There are many legends of those malicious things. Let us not dwell on them. What do we expect to happen between these continents of Magyther, Torem and the Tyranlands? It shall be violent no matter what."

"Whatever passes between them we shall be forced to take sides. Or rather, not. When the time comes for us to give this sword away, we must give it to one who shall bring peace to the world, rather than causing peace through unfixable, terrible violence. And do not forget: there are unexplored and unclaimed islands between here and the North that may hold unholy threats that could bring all the continents together, preventing peace for a short while but forcing peace afterwards."

"I do think it unlikely, Brother. These islands you speak of have likely already been taken over by the Tyrans, as most are near the Tyrans. So, it must be that we find the One to wield the sword, who is powerful enough to take war and wage war on it, ending war with war and rather bringing peace." The two men stopped riding as they saw smoke in the near distance.

"And what is this smoke? If it is Dusk Hill set ablaze, then I, alas, shall be without a place to call my old home."

"Let us ride, then! Let us discover!"

It had been hours since the violent assault on Henry's war camp. King Henry was exploding,

"Who was that archer!? Who!? Who!? You wreck of a near-dead man, I will grind your bones and your brain into a disgusting mixture that we shall pour upon the heads of our attackers. Who, bloody who!? I know, you, Louis, have a family. I shall track them all down and have them hung before you as you die if you do not tell me who the archer was who spread chaos through our ranks, killed many of us and helped free you and two other prisoners! IT HAS CAUSED CHAOS!! WE DO NOT FEAR THIS CHAOS, BUT YOU SHALL PAY DEARLY IF YOU DO NOT TELL US!!"

"Why, then. His name? Eric. But you do not know him."

"Thank you, sir." The King of Rosewick drew his sword and carved the head of Louis in half. "The name of your Crimson Archer who you fear so, soldiers, is Eric."

"I knew Eric! I met him once! And he was an archer!" shouted one soldier.

"Tell me more, soldier."

"He lived in the Grayewoods. The Master huntsman's apprentice, he was. But he was due to finish his apprenticeship recently. He has likely moved away from the Grayewoods now." said the same soldier.

"I knew all of that already, soldier. But thank you for your time. It shall be difficult to locate this traitor, and we cannot have many men looking for him. We shall choose ten of you to pursue and kill him and those he is travelling with. Who here volunteers?" said King Henry as many, many hands raised about the crowd.

"You! Tall man! Come up to the stage and raise your sword to the skies!"

"You! Ugly brute! Come up to the stage and raise your sword to the skies!"

"You! Stout one! Come up to the stage and raise your sword to the skies!"

"You! Axe-bearer! Come up to the stage and raise your axe to the skies!"

"You! Grinning one! Come up to the stage and raise your sword to the skies!"

"You! You! You! You! And You! You five, come up to the stage and raise your swords to the skies. We have lost ten good soldiers today, men. But these ten heroes shall avenge the deaths of those other brave soldiers who died fighting a traitor. Cheer for the dead!! Cheer for the survivors!! Cheer for those who shall strike with vengeance!!"

Cheers, clapping and shouts once again echoed around Torem Coast.

*   *   *

Eric, Elaina, Thomas and Edward had made it far from Torem Coast. They all had their own horses now; they had stopped briefly at a small village to visit the stables earlier that morning.

"We need to find a small town where people will not recognise us. If possible, a village."

"Then I have a recommendation!" said Edward excitedly. "My cousin's cousin's uncle on me mum's side had a carrot selling business down at the farming village Dusk Hill. T'snot too far from 'ere; we may as well pay that innocent village a visit."

"We shall not get there tonight - but we may as well head there. Alright, we shall go, Edward."

"We need to head South fer Dusk Hill. 'Tis one of the villages closest to the southern Forests - which we can easily escape into if we are attacked."

"Again, a good tactical location, Edward. But we must find a place to stay before we reach there: it should take about two to three days to reach Dusk Hill."

"Good reasoning, Eric. We must find a town. We cannot even think of going near Castle Wormwood - that would be far too obvious…" Thomas was suddenly interrupted by Eric.

"Actually, the villages near Castle Wormwood may be our best bet. Think about it. If it would be so tactically poor to go there, then nobody would suspect it. So we must go there. For our own sakes."

"You really think that's a good idea? I think not."

"Think about it more, Thomas. Those who are following us shall be cunning. They shall not expect us, of course, to be stupid deliberately. In the same way, they would not expect us to allow them to capture us freely."

"So be it. I shall regret this…" Thomas said grimly. As he said so, they began heading straight for Castle Wormwood.

"We shall make sure you do not, Thomas. If Arora becomes Queen again, soldiers who helped her would surely be amply rewarded. Edward, too. Me, too. And somehow Elaina would be rewarded, too."

"Wait, Elaina? Princess Elaina of Starbill? Mate, ye'v been traveling with a bloody rich princess! Haven't yer bloody made yer move yet?" whispered Thomas quietly to Eric.

"No..? Do you expect me to? I've never been the one to do such a thing. It has always been you, Edward and Louis… But perhaps I shall at some point. She is pretty. And confident. And intelligent. And capable."

"Glad to see you've erected some interest. We'll talk more later."

Chapter Nine

CRIMSON DAWN

It was past midday, and the two monks had not yet reached the source of smoke.

"Oh Lord, fire! Horrible, horrible fire! Bodies! Screams! Shouts! I see many shapes moving. Wicked embers of heat consuming that innocent village! From atop this tree I do, alas, spy Dusk Hill." Kai had climbed a tree to see in the distance Dusk Hill set aflame.

"Lord, purge this red dawn of death that has set itself upon the destruction of such a pure place! Should I write a history of that lovely place, I would never cope with myself while I wrote its fateful ending."

"That bad? The village in ashes…" Dak was standing at the bottom of the tree, waiting till his fellow monk came down.

"There is time, to prevent this. Let us go and help!" said Kai slowly. "Yes. There is time to prevent this." Kai then fell from the tree, sailing down through the billowing air and smashing front-down onto the spring forest floor.

Dak flipped the limp monk to his front. He then decided that Kai had survived far worse. Only a little blood was coming from his nose. Dak doubted that the ex-warrior would be without wounds, but he left the man on the floor and instead went to help the village. It would have been what the monk would have wanted, anyway. But what he found was that the village was being attacked. He saw a great deal of raiders dressed in sandy clothes and wielding scimitars torching the place and looting the houses. Many citizens were tied up in the centre of the village as Dak could see from outside, and a few bodies next to them showed that there had been some casualties as well. Dak immediately returned to his stirring friend, who he shook awake. "You fell from the tree. You have been out for twenty minutes. But, I have made an important discovery. The town was not set alight by natural causes. Raiders, by the looks of things of origin from Magyther, are stealing everything the villagers have, tying them up in the centre of the village, and killing others."

"No!! No!!" Kai stood up in seconds and drew the sword in his scabbard: Dragontongue. "Those bastards shall die!!" He leapt upon the horse that had been nibbling at grass for a half-hour and rode up the hill that was the namesake of the village.

"Ah, wait for me, Brother." Dak clambered onto his horse in a less hasty way and made it his objective to catch up with his fellow monk. He rose over the hill and saw Kai speeding up to the village, Dragontongue already in his grip.

*   *   *

Ten men rode on the fastest horses that could be found for them. They had near-empty saddlebags and were all travelling with such speed that they would easily catch up with their targets. The main noticeable thing about the ten riders was that they all wore glimmering steel armour and carried sharpened weapons on their belts. They were clearly soldiers, and spread strange feelings of fear through all they passed on the road. They asked everyone they encountered along the way if they had seen four people pass through. Every now and then they did so hear of where their elusive targets were, sometimes they thought that the ones they were asking were telling lies, for they did not catch a single glimpse of the ones they were pursuing till that evening of their first day of riding. It had felt like years since they had left the camp, and they only found them by pure luck. They were riding along a path quickly and then, when they turned round a bend covered by trees, they found the dangerous traitors they were seeking. Four riders all upon their own horses, travelling slowly. The ten soldiers sped up, drawing their weapons. But seeing them, the four bashed their heels against their horses' sides and began galloping quicker as well. Who they truly underestimated was the one they recognised as the archer who had attacked an entire army of soldiers, who spat an arrow at them via his fine longbow and killed straight one of the ten's numbers.

"The ten are now nine!" The archer shouted over the din of galloping and shouts.

"Good job Eric, you saved us! Oh wait! There are still nine of them!" Thomas had once again swayed to the cynical side of things, focusing on the fact that they were being chased by nine armed and dangerous soldiers. Edward rode onwards without looking back. Then, he noticed that his saddlebags were empty. He detached them in the blink of an eye and threw them at the men who were charging at them from behind, the bags gently bashing them and one covering a horse's eye. The said horse shook its head wildly, and reared backwards and onto its back legs, half-throwing its rider from his leather saddle. With all the commotion in the soldiers' ranks, they slowed and helped their allies back onto their horses, except in the case of the dead man and the free horse which were decorating the road. They lost track of their targets in the maze of trees at a junction, in which went two directions: one to Castle Wormwood and the other to the countryside. Of course, the soldiers assumed that the other riders had headed through the countryside. They were wrong.

"We have lost them! A good idea of yours, Eric, to go through here. I take back what I said about this plan. They fell for it like flightless birds." said Thomas with newfound optimism.

"Well, that's all we can say for now. They would have been able to see us in the countryside out there. Once they actually reach it, they shall turn back and come after us. However, they shall be too late and we shall be long gone. Unless we are slowed here by an unforeseen hazard."

"Don't tempt the Lord, Eric. He'd take any chance to screw us over." said Edward scornfully.

"Oh yes, don't tempt the Lord, Eric. Edward's right. Probably. But who knows? Oh wait, the Lord knows. He knows whether he'll screw us up or not. But resist the Lord! Be clever! Try to foresee the strange things that could happen to us."

"Ok. Number One; Suddenly we are ambushed, and are all killed or captured." said Edward.

"See! That won't happen now." said Thomas.

"I know, right?" replied Edward.

"I was being sarcastic. Please do not list the ways we could die or be captured."

"Number Two. I continue with these and Thomas gets angry!" shouted Edward.

"Well, now that you've shouted like that they're likely to find us again. Well done!" Eric ended the conversation brutally. Thomas then pulled up to the side of Eric.

"So you're pretending to be a tough guy for the Princess, eh? I can get more annoyed with Edward, and you can constantly defuse our squabbling."

"I have said before, Thomas, you need not say or do anything. I have my own situation under control."

"I guess you do not need my help for your excellent skills in lady wooing."

"Shut up, Thomas. You're speaking louder and louder."

"I guess if you don't like her, then I'll go after her." replied Thomas. As he spoke, Edward sped to the side of Eric as well.

"Nah. You can't. You have to follow the Pact. We all swore to it, remember? One of us sees a lady who we're interested in? Whoever saw first gets the first dibs to go after her. Eric may be the smooth-talker and handsome man first in this case. For now, me and Thomas shall slather our faces in mud every morning to make ourselves as ugly as possible. Then, you'll look way better next to us."

"Very funny, Edward. But, do nothing. These times are dangerous and are not for messing around. We are likely to have wanted posters showing our names in many places around here soon. So, we cannot draw too much attention to ourselves with shouting and chatter."

"You're right. We were to be executed. Louis is dead, or dying. Or in great pain. Our Queen has been reduced to a prisoner. Our new monarch one who would hunt us down and kill us himself if he could. We are indeed in a bad spot."

*   *   *

Adrenaline had taken over Dai-No-Kai's veins. As he felt the tense flesh of the raiders being sliced and shredded beneath the huge but light Dragontongue, his inner soldier screamed with intensity. He was killing once again! He was hopelessly outnumbered but was not afraid. Dak had come to his side with a bamboo staff to bludgeon the small brains of the Magithan raiders who wielded the double scimitars that so continued to miss the bodies of the two monks, who seemed to see the whole battle as slow motion. But such immunity did not last for the two monks. Dak, as fast as his staff strikes were, was cleanly stabbed in his side. Gushing blood came through the wound, and the disagreeable gnome-slayer was grounded to the hot grass in agony. Kai fell a few seconds later, his guard faltering even with the magical aid of the legendary sword. His shoulder was sliced deeply, and he, too, fell. The two monks were tied minutes later alongside the rest of the citizens, who had watched the fight in horror. The fire began to rage on outside of the limits that most had seen in their lifetimes. "We have no need of you people, and we shall not kill you. However, we shall make you watch your own town burn so that you know that coming after the Volo Raiders would be useless. And you two. You two monks.

Your Lord shall laugh at your hilarious attempt to stop this. And I thought those of the Dynasty considered fighting a sin." The raider who had spoken then sported a hoarse, dry and sour laugh which made Dai-No-Kai cringe with anger. The raiders ran off minutes later after gathering themselves and checking who was dead.

"Of course it was Dusk Hill. Bad fates only seem to reach us, Brother. First the gnomes and the wraiths, then the abandoned mercenaries' place, then this. This horrible occurrence. The Lord is unhappy with me, I know it. I have become too much of a warrior again. But I was not warrior enough to save this place."

"You must choose, Kai. Monk or warrior. You can be either but not both. Unless, of course, you receive special blessing from the Lord to do so."

"I do not think I will, brother. I have not been favoured a great deal yet. It is not unusual for two unorthodox monks to have bad luck."

"Usually because they are unorthodox: torn between what they feel they need to do and what the Lord commands them to do. Their interpretations of the Lord's commands change things as well."

"The Lord gives equal luck to those who are not religious as well. Perhaps the fate the Lord has given us is simply of beginning with bad luck. There is still plenty of room for victory and happiness."

"Perhaps, Kai. Perhaps."

*   *   *

"Those filthy Tyrans are only three days away. Soon to be only two. And yet I am not worried at all! It is as if the Lord has granted me infinite confidence and bravery!" said King Henry as he spoke with his skeleton crew of advisors.

"It is good, sire, that you are not worried. However, there are a few small problems. Too much bravery is foolishness! We are not being ruled by a fool? But if we were, I must say, a good fool to be a leader." King Henry's newest head advisor was an opinionated priest, and Henry was already beginning to dislike him.

"I am not going to become foolish, priest. I am not afraid of them, that is all. And were you saying that it would be wise to be afraid of them? Are you saying that the odds are in their favour? I should hope that the last advisor who I truly trust I can still trust? Or perhaps you are thinking it would be better to switch sides and find our weaknesses at the last second to save your own skin. If you attempt to do so, I shall have your 'saved' skin decorating my wall."

"Of course not, sire. Please do not skin me. I am still useful to you I'm sure."

"I grow bored, priest. Amuse me. Throw yourself off these cliffs if you will: it shall be funny to test if bodies are ripped apart by those sharp rocks below. Because, if they are, we'll mine them off and use them as defences."

"My King? Are you going quite mad? How would we use them as defences? How would we attach them to anything?"

"And now you are calling me mad quite like that late King Vorodin. Oh dear. It does seem that this pathetic advisor thinks he can challenge the will of the King! The King that can execute him immediately! The King that holds all the power! The King that could command his soldiers to impale anyone with their wonderfully sharp swords. You call me mad? Mad?"

"N-no, sire -" The priest spoke but he was too late to undo what he said, and was grabbed by the throat with the two cold hands of King Henry. He was then thrown to the ground. "You are out of place, servant. I shall not kill you now, but any signs of this again shall result in your death."

"O-o-of course, m-my King."

"Not good enough. Swear by the Lord of the Afterlife if you will; swear by your own life if you will; swear by Rosewick if you will."

"I d-do swear by the health of my King that I shall not turn traitor."

"And how indeed do you intend to get out of this swear? By having assassins kill me?"

"I would never -"

"Leave me, priest. I will know, however, if you plan to kill me. And I shall end you before you end me. For I am not at all mad, foolish or useless as you see me."

*   *   *

The four travellers had arrived in the village of Grukh-Mol inconspicuously. They had donned black cloaks before they had entered, and quickly blended into the crowd of farmers, children and others who were cloaked in similar ways.

"I spy an Inn that we may find useful. It looks relatively unpopular so there will be space for us to sleep, and not many who are of high status will be in there, making it less likely that anybody will recognise Elaina." Eric pointed to a ramshackle building with a sign half hanging off it saying The Newt's Tail Inn.

"That one's obviously crap. Why do we have to go there?" asked Edward.

"I just explained why. Those there will be poor and will be completely lost in their drinks, not even noticing us enter. It adds an element of stealth for us through this town." replied Eric.

"I thought we were staying at this one? This is near Castle Wormwood."

"It is, but not near enough. It's also far away enough for people to think we've fled here. One night we shall stay." said Elaina. At this Edward grumbled.

"More travelling and sleeping in a bad Inn? Worst. Day. Ever."

"You could have been executed instead, if you would have preferred."

"Eric's right, Edward. I, Thomas, would rather live than die publicly. It's my own choice. I think most people would agree with me."

"Fine. We'll stay at the bloody cauldron of an Inn and we'll have rats scurrying across our faces all night and bats swooping around above us."

"Yep. Sounds like a nice social experience, doesn't it?"

They tethered their horses outside the Inn and ventured inside. Within they found a dingy, damp and smelly bar at which hardly any stools were taken. A gruff man was behind it.

"Welcome to the Newt's Tail Inn. How may I help you?"

"Any rooms available, good sir?"

"All rooms available, sir. All rooms. Take your pick, if you have enough gold."

"And how much gold does each standard room cost?"

"Six per night."

"What the bloody hell? This is overpricing. Let us 'ave a bloody fricking look at these pigsties first."

"Seven for rude ones. Eight for rich ones. Twenty for arseholes. Six for decent folk. You, mate, have been increased to seven."

"We only have thirteen gold. So Edward, don't get too angry. We need these rooms. And keep in mind that the other Inns would be more expensive."

"Well then. You can get two rooms if yer pay me all that money. Costs extra because of that nasty one."

"How many beds are in each room?"

"One one-and-a-half size bed in each room."

"You, Edward, may sleep on the floor. I'll take the bed." said Thomas.

"But that's assuming that Eric will be in the same room as Elaina!" whispered Edward loudly.

"Eric saw first, remember? You're the one who reminded us of 'the pact'." whispered Thomas back.

"Ugh… Fine." replied Edward.

"Hey, Eric and Elaina. We were thinking: since you saved us from being executed, you two can choose a room first." said Thomas.

"Now you're letting them choose first as well?" hissed Edward.

"I accept. Eric?"

"Okay. I don't mind having first pick. And don't worry, you've thanked us enough. Don't feel the need to worship us." Eric and Elaina went up the stairs. Minutes later Edward and Thomas followed, walking into a random room. The floor was wet and had unthinkable things littered on it: empty pouches, marbles, clothing and other strange decorations such as shattered plates and bloodied cutlery. The bed's cloth was black and had dust covering its sheets. As the silence continued, the bartender entered the room.

"Ah, our second finest standard room. Are you taking this one? I have already received your payment from your friends."

"Of course we are!" Said Thomas stepping into the room and onto shards of a smashed wine bottle.

"I'll leave you two to discuss who goes where." The bartender closed the door behind him as he left.

"You are a dick, Thomas. Look at this bloody floor! It is literally bloody! Stained with things I don't want to know about, smashed things everywhere, spiderwebs with large arachnids dangling from the ceiling. The room's lock is broken. The floor is the worst part! There's even a dead rat over there. And right here is a shredded shirt. Many, many things have happened in this room."

"It's good to be in a nice, historical place," Thomas laid on top of the bed, then shouted. "Bloody hell! There's something moving under those sheets!" He sprung up from the bed, and threw off the sheets. Underneath were two rats and a den of straw and other random things.

"Disgusting. Two mating rats stuffed under dusty bedsheets. You know, I'm wondering if Eric and Elaina are having similar problems."

"Nah. I bet their room is walled with gold and has huge windows."

"Yeah, right. Maybe we should go to another Inn and get a few drinks."

"Agreed, agreed! Let us leave this horrid place."

CHAPTER TEN

CRIMSON TWILIGHT

All that was left of Dusk Hill was before Dak and
Dai-No-Kai. They had freed themselves from their
ropes ten minutes before and the wounds that could
be helped had been helped, but they had not escaped
quickly enough to save any remnants of the village. A
few blackened and unwieldy planks remained of a few
houses, in some cases a pot or a vase or a few coins
were spared. Otherwise, ashes were all that remained
of the small village. The fire had even spread to the
farmers' crops: the corn had been popped, then been
roasted unpleasantly. Nothing remained of the wheat.
In the same way, nothing remained of the potatoes
the farmers had been so proud of save a single small
plant which was withering with malnutrition. A few
of the farmers had also tried to resist the raiders, and
they had been left for dead in the fire. Alongside the
smell of burnt wood there was also the smell of
burnt flesh. Dai-No-Kai had taken the blame and
pinned it on himself. In fact, all the people tied up

seemed to be powerless till the town was fully burnt down: it was as if they were held in place to watch. In the same way, the two monks had watched till no embers of flame remained, at the dark time of evening.

"By the Lord, these people are suffering. And you too, Kai. We need to get you - and them - out of here. 'Tis too much of a grim place for rest."

"Why could it not rain, Dak? Why could salvation not come from the clouds? Why indeed did these raiders come? Filthy Magithan scum, always raiding other lands for food and water."

"They do what they need to do. Those deserts that take up half of their lands are hot and have no such lakes as we have here. Wells, I heard, would be useless as well: Cacti eat up all the water in the sand and soil below the surface. If they could, they would conquer this place and live here as well."

"And they have not conquered it, thus they instead take small, important parts back to their own lands, the lands that nobody wanted, and consume them. I do hate Magithans - I was almost killed in a war against them. And now they have burnt down the only home I knew, save the decaying temples in the southern mountains. Everybody is ruthless - everybody is sour and everybody sins. It is unavoidable, so people focus on themselves: they keep themselves alive so that they may commit even more sins in this world. Ruin even more pure land with mouldy houses and violent wars. And they do not care what they are doing to this world! We created Wraiths, those villains who kill us and reap our souls and do every sinful act that they could possibly glisten from their stupid existence. The Goblins and Trolls. If we had united, we could have stopped them. The Gnomes, however, have no fault in this. They are a perfect civilisation: they adapt to the land, and do not force the land to adapt to them. They take care of the land: they fix abandoned ruins to be simple places for nature to slowly reclaim. Ah, the Lord loves the Gnomes. All the gods - as I believe that belief creates - love the Gnomes for protecting the one realm they created."

"You have sunk deep into your emotions, brother." said Dak slowly. "But, we must leave this place. It is in wicked shadowy ruins like this that Wraiths do take their wicked second-lives."

"Brother, you need not take care of me - but take

care of the people of Dusk Hill if you will." Dai-No-Kai turned from the blackened remains of the village and walked slowly away, briefly calling back "Have them follow us. We shall reach the next town along the journey to Castle Wormwood with a day's march, and we can camp in these meadows that have barely escaped the fire. As you said, Dak. There is still time in our lives for victory and happiness."

"Dai-No-Kai? Do you still have Dragontongue in your scabbard? I only just remembered the sword."

"Aye, brother. Catch up, will you? We must leave, as you said."

"Kai, the people do not want to leave, it is their home. They want to rebuild. It is only natural for them."

"You know, Dak, I found it difficult to leave this place when I was enlisted to the army. Perhaps I could stay; you could take the sword to whoever must wield it."

"A pilgrimage must be finished, Dai-No-Kai. You must come: I am not a warrior, I cannot defend myself. Sure, I have been known to fend off one or two attackers with my staff, but you have capability in battle. You must come with me for only together we can complete this journey."

147

"Ah, Dak. Your consultation helps. It shall be painful knowing my people will be forced to rebuild with their pockets empty, but I shall come with you. For our mission is for the wellbeing of the entire South, including Dusk Hill and its residents."

"Peace shall come quicker now that we are both going. We shall 'be swift!'."

*   *   *

"So now there are increased reports of Magithans raiding small towns and villages nearer the coast. Can you tell me a few of the victims?"

"Er, Dusk Hill is in ashes, your majesty."

"Dusk Hill is a small farming village far beneath our notice. Have they struck anywhere important?"

"Your majesty, this may be concerning: they have raided your home, Norlick."

"And why have they not attacked villages in Starbill?" said King Henry angrily.

"Well, your majesty, we have far more supplies everywhere. Starbill is smaller, as well, so they find it easier to spread out their troops. They have soldiers at each and every village and town."

"Why us, then? Those Magithan raiders can handle a few soldiers. And Starbill is between them and us. In fact, they're an entire ocean and a Starbill from us!"

"Your majesty, they've not just passed through Starbill to get to us. They have sailed the other way. A relatively long sea journey but one that still works and brings them straight to us. And so I can tell you: Norlick was raided. Of course, as a larger town, its garrison defended it. We don't think anybody important to you died, but -"

"I care not for my old dukedom or for any of the people who live there. I am assuming they haven't come this far North - they have not yet attacked Halcore, correct? I believe the place has, however, been on lockdown since Duke Gallance's death."

"Correct, your majesty. They're still attempting to discover who killed him. Awful dagger marks. Very bloody, I heard."

"Ah, yes. Poor Gallance. But changing the subject, I think we may have to wage war on Magyther again after this event with the Tyrans has ended. For they are becoming a thorn I cannot cope with."

"And perhaps we shall, if they survive, be able to enlist the help of Starbill. They sport a dislike of the

Magithans in the same way. Either that, or they shall team up with the Magithans against us. But your majesty, I believe your idea shall come to be used. Eventually."

*　　　*　　　*

Thomas and Edward had snuck out of the Newt's Tail Inn as quickly as they could - the smell had begun to make their noses be permanently wrinkled. They had made their way from the shack to yet another Inn, this time labelled the Wraith's Soul Inn. It was in a much better state of repair than the previous Inn, rather sporting the stale smells of bread and wine, only a bit of mould and only a couple of dead rats. They claimed themselves seats at the bar and began to relax.

"'Ey, bartender. Pour me a mugga ale, will 'ya?" Edward immediately grabbed the mug that was offered to him and poured the liquid down his throat. Thomas, however, was more careful.

"A mug of ale, please."

"Of course, sir." Thomas was handed a mug that was perhaps more full than the one Edward had been given. He took a gentle sip of the frothing liquid and nearly sputtered.

"This isn't bloody ale!?" he whispered to Edward, who had already gotten another mug.

"Isn't it?"

"No! No! No! Tastes like bloody swamp water! And that's not what it's supposed to taste like!"

"Well, in my experience, it does -"

"That's because you get drunk the moment you take a single sip, Edward. Things get strange. Anyway, I reckon this guy's a scammer. Aren't there any good Inns in this bloody town?"

The Bartender chipped in,

"I'm a scammer, am I? Boys, get in here!" Two huge men came from a door behind the bar, both with clubs in their hands. "So, still think I'm a scammer? Still think my ale tastes like swamp water, eh? You will put off my customers! I have a reputation around here! A reputation for killing those I do not like, eh? Who here agrees that I kill those I don't like? Raise your mugs!"

All the customers raised their mugs as quickly as they could.

"You see? You stop putting off my customers, or I

kill you and take the money you owe me from your corpse. In fact, you owe me one gold. Do you have a gold, or are you thieves who thought you could scam the one you called a scammer! You wanted to trick the great Ralph Von Triili, eh? Clap clap, gentlemen. You shall never scam again, eh? Boys, get them!" Edward and Thomas both jumped from their seats as clubs were swung towards their heads.

"Ah, resistors! But you shall still die, eh?"

"Edward, we have no weapons! How are you with your fists?"

"I've never fought in a street fight before! I've never fought hand-to-hand before!" Thomas did not respond to Edward, rather grabbing the club of one of the men and yanking it from his hand, and then passing it to Edward.

"Thanks." as Edward thanked Thomas, he bashed the chest of one of the men in front of them, causing the lump of muscle and fat to stumble backwards. Thomas then punched and winded the weaponless man via a hard gut punch. The man subsequently fell to the ground. The other combatant, then outnumbered, was bashed in the balls by Edward as he was punched in the nose by Thomas.

"Still think we are scammers, Triili?" asked Thomas.

"No. Maybe you can pay me back another time, eh? You need not pay me now, feel free to leave if you do not like my service, eh?"

"Yes. We shall be leaving now, Triili. And by the way, we don't like you. And our reputation around other parts is we kill those we don't like. We'll be back at some point, Triili."

"Ah yes, I see." The small bartender gulped. Thomas and Edward returned to the Newt's Tail Inn and eventually found comfort on the ground of the second floor corridor. The next morning, the four travellers woke up early to head South.

"We may make it past Castle Wormwood today. In fact, we woke up so early we may get more than three-quarters of the way to Dusk Hill from here to there."

"Good! My cousin's cousin's uncle awaits!"

"Who exactly is he, by the way." asked Thomas.

"Well, his name - I think - is Dai-No-Kai. Apparently he fought a war against the Magithans when he was young, then he became a monk. Apparently every year or so he comes down to Dusk Hill. So we might not see him."

"But, you told us he has a carrot farming business!"

"I told you he had a carrot farming business. He only did before the war." responded Edward.

"Great. The one man who could have given us accommodation in the place we're headed may or may not be there."

*   *   *

Dak and Dai-No-Kai had managed to leave the village behind. Their horses had been slain in the battle against the raiders, thus they were travelling slowly and on foot. Their day had consisted of pure uneventful travelling, and it was getting to evening. "I see four riders coming our way, Dai-No-Kai."

"Let them come. They do not look too dangerous."

As their two paths crossed, the riders paused.

"Are you headed for Dusk Hill, travellers? There is nothing else along this road."

"Yes. Why?" answered a man with a quiver of arrows and a bow on his back.

"Sad days for you, then. Dusk Hill has been burnt to ashes - the people are alive and will be rebuilding, but they shall not be finished for a long time."

"And do you know if a man named Dai-No-Kai was in the village at the time, travellers?"

"Yes. He was. And he is standing before you now. This is Dak." said Dai-No-Kai, pointing to his companion.

"Our names are Ella, Eric, Edward and Thomas. Edward is your relative, somehow."

"Indeed! Greetings! You're my cousin's cousin's uncle."

"I... have bad news for you. My brother died a year ago - perhaps you had already heard."

"Yes, my cousin's cousin's father died. But, however, you, are alive! How goes it, Brother?"

"My fellow monk Dak and I are on a pilgrimage to deliver a great weapon -"

"Shut up, Dai-No-Kai! We don't know if we can trust these people!"

"If you are outside all the factions in the world, we are your allies." said Eric.

"We want peace - and none of the factions of the world save the Dynasty want that. But even we are unorthodox members of the Dynasty. So you may call us your allies."

"Peace, huh? The world cannot have peace without

leaders who are capable of it. New leadership seems to be required... everywhere. But yes, we can agree that peace is ideal for this world." said Thomas.

"Ah, fellow lovers of the great Peace. I think we can trust these people, Dak. Our mission is to find a worthy wielder of the great sword Dragontongue, crafted by perhaps the greatest Gnomish smith in the world - Durbain - and brought into our hands by Baledor, son of Durbain. Dragontongue is destined for a user who can find peace or make peace with all creatures, by ending them or by making them their ally. One who could defeat a dragon without drawing his weapon, by simply reaching an agreement with it. And we have yet to even find anybody who wants peace. But you have filled out lots of criteria."

"Dai-No-Kai, you made up half of that stuff -"

"Shh, I want to hear the rest." said Edward. Dak rolled his eyes.

"Has anyone here ever looked upon a Drake or Dragon and not felt the need to run, hide or fight?"

"Eric has. I watched with my own eyes as he made a deal with a Drake for safe passage through its territory."

"Eric, are your shoulders ready for a burden? An

unimaginably large and heavy burden?"

"I already have the burden of ending the lives of evil men on my shoulders, and the burden of being a wanted man on my shoulders. I have survived as of yet. If I must take another burden, I shall not flinch with the weight."

"Eric, you could be a hero! A great damned hero! Why haven't I bloody encountered a bloody Drake?"

"Because Edward, you would scream and run away. I believe you would find the experience - if you had it - rather traumatising." said Thomas.

"Eric, do you have the potential to be a leader?"

"I would say so: he was the leader when, me, Edward, Eric and Louis went drinking."

"Eric, do you have the potential to have control?"

"I do. It takes control to aim and fire a bow, which I have done thousands of times. You are not considering giving the sword to me, are you?"

"Oh, no. We are not considering giving it to you. We are giving it to you." Dai-No-Kai drew the sword from his scabbard and placed it in Eric's open hands.

"You're not giving the sword to somebody we just met, are you? You are still recovering from the shock of the fire, and the fall..."

"It feels right, Dak. It feels like… fate."

"Dai-No-Kai. Dak. The sword… it feels as if it was crafted for my own hands."

"You see, Dak? My point is proven. And Eric, there is a matching pair of armour. We would give it to you now, but plate armour takes time to put on."

"Are we turning back now, Kai?"

"No, Dak. We are going to help these people get to Torem Coast once again and bring peace to the world!"

A thunder of sudden hoofbeats clattered through the silence, perking up the ears of all at the gathering. Nine soldiers in full armour and wielding huge weapons all riding large, fast steeds came round a bend in the road that curved around the trees like a maze, suddenly appearing in the view of the six travellers. Eric leapt back onto his horse and Edward pulled Dai-No-Kai up with him. Thomas pulled Dak up onto his horse and began to ride away as he was followed by Edward and Elaina. Edward and Thomas, weaponless, were fleeing, and Elaina was following them. Eric twirled Dragontongue in his grip, and charged forwards on his horse, straight away carving through the thick flesh of one of the surprised soldiers.

"Eric! You cannot fight nine - oh, one's dead - eight - soldiers on horseback!" shouted Thomas to his friend who was in the thick of the battle.

"No. This I can do."

Character Index:

HUNTSMEN:

Eric: A cunning and precise archer of eighteen years of age, Eric is a huntsman and is soon to graduate from his apprenticeship with Frederick the Master huntsman of the Grayewoods. Eric is loyal, good and kind, but sometimes battle takes him into a frenzy, and he becomes brutal.

Frederick: The Master huntsman of the Grayewoods. He is a hunter but a tamer of beasts, a killer but a friend of the forest and its systems. He can find all in the Grayewoods and can identify any tracks. He is extremely deadly with knives and bows, and has great skill in combat. However, he is reluctant to battle other human beings. The huntsman is the Master of his apprentice, Eric. Many fear him for his skill, but soon learn after truly meeting him that his soul is good and kind.

ROYAL FAMILY OF ROSEWICK:

Queen Arora: The sad and pregnant Queen Arora is undisciplined in the art of leadership, but is very willing to learn with opportunities. She is somewhat unpopular as a leader with Duke Gallance and Duke Henry. Arora is kind, giving and sensitive.

James II: Fondly remembered as the best King of Rosewick in recent times, James II laid siege to Starbill for six months. But as his troops had grown so tired and exhausted, he returned to Rosewick, defeated. But on his warpath he had two great allies with him: his trusted Duke Gallance and the young, excellent strategist who was the heir to a dukedom. His name was Henry. He also laid siege to Magyther with the same two men. James II desperately wanted to live till the Tyrans finally invaded to be killed in battle, but the winter brought colds and eventually, after a long struggle, fever claimed his soul without honour. King Mortimer succeeded him on the throne of Rosewick.

King Mortimer: The brave King Mortimer is embarked upon a mission to assassinate the great King-Emperor Kaldorn of the North. A valiant warrior, a son of James II and the husband of Queen Arora, Mortimer is a brave man and an excellent strategist. However, none believe he shall come back alive from his mission. Mortimer is extremely charitable and defensive of his allies.

DUKES OF ROSEWICK:

Duke Henry: A bitter man who served alongside James II in the Starbillian War against the people of Starbill, Duke Henry ravaged the lands of his enemies and killed the wife of the King of Starbill. Hated strongly by the Prince of Starbill, Isaak, he is well known among Rosewick and is generally disliked by all but the Dukes of Rosewick. Henry is middle-aged, a decent fighter and an extremely clever strategist, however he uses his gifts only for himself.

Duke Gallance: Another bitter man who also served in the Starbillian War alongside Duke Henry. However, Gallance was a veteran in those times - and is now an elderly man. Duke Gallance looks out mainly for himself but has a strong sense of nationalism, wanting the best for his kingdom, Rosewick, as well.

TYRANS:

King-Emperor Kaldorn: The huge, brutish hulk Kaldorn has many titles, all of which make his enemies quiver in their boots. Accomplisher of great things, he conquered the entire North side of the world - and intends to conquer the southern half as soon as the chilling winter has ended. Kaldorn is the absolute best warrior in the world, an incredible fighter but dull tactician. He wears the Hark Crown proudly and his own title he had made for himself is 'Kaldorn, Harklord'.

Son-of-Kaldorn Bniir: Known commonly as 'Bniir Silvertongue', Bniir speaks well and is a greater strategist than even the likes of Duke Henry and many past King-Emperors. Bniir is often thought of as the most likely Son-of-Kaldorn to become the next King-Emperor.

Son-of-Kaldorn Istulgruf: Known commonly as 'Istulgruf The Conqueror', Istulgruf is a strategist decently capable of cunning battle and is also an excellent fighter. Between Bniir and Marka in all ways, Istulgruf is the most favoured by Kaldorn.

Son-of-Kaldorn Marka: Known commonly as 'Dragon Bane Marka', Marka's size is unrivalled among Tyrans. He has no tactics for his battle but to make up for his lack of intelligence, his strength and fortitude are twice that of an elephant.

ROYAL FAMILY OF STARBILL:

King Vorodin: Known hardly ever as Vorodin, the King of Starbill is mad and has been touched by a very potent wraith. Roughly once per day he returns to sanity to utter a few words, but otherwise he is a gibbering lunatic.

Princess Elaina: A beautiful woman surrounded by suitors, Elaina is confident and powerful without being brutal. Her words are her weapons and she wields them well, cutting wounds no such blade could draw. She is the daughter of the King of Starbill, and is the twin of Prince Isaak. She was born only minutes after him.

Prince Isaak: Many tell legends of how Isaak's heart is made of ice and snow. His demeanour so cold and his tone so violent, Isaak is opposed by his opposite twin: Elaina. He has no empathy nor sympathy for any that suffer save himself. He is a strong and competent fighter.

HIGH-RANKING MEMBERS OF THE ROSEWICK ARMY:

Sir Rusga: The greatest knight of Halcore is the half-brother of Battlemaster Voss, a drillmaster of Castle Wormwood. Rusga is a very thickly-muscled brute of indomitable strength and vitality. He is ruthless, enjoys combat and furthermore takes pleasure in the pain of others. Certain people Rusga takes a very strong hatred to.

Battlemaster Voss: The most difficult drillmaster to endure. The hard-pressing trainer trains a segment of the army of Rosewick, including the soldiers Thomas, Edward and Louis, who he has taken a particular hatred to. Voss hates with passion and will stop at nothing to inflict pain or even death on those he hates.

SOLDIERS:

Thomas: Friend of Edward, Louis and Eric, Thomas is a loyal friend. He is an excellent soldier and with proper training could become a true warrior. But with only a mean, unfair teacher such as Battlemaster Voss, he is still lacking in experience and skill, and talent is all he has.

Louis: The drunkard Louis gets annoyed quickly. However, his fierce temper has proved useful in combat. On the occasion his friends are in true danger, Louis does act, but begrudgingly if it makes him risk his own life. A bit arrogant and greedy, Louis enjoys getting Thomas annoyed - but sometimes goes too far. Otherwise, he is a large, strong soldier.

Edward: Edward is often seen as the average young soldier. He drinks to look tough, he's not confident enough to talk to ladies and he's a fighter that could easily be felled in battle by a larger or more skilled opponent. However, his strong friends Louis, Eric and Thomas often protect him.

MONKS:

Brother Dak: A relatively youthful monk, Dak is growing into his wisdom but not growing out of his insolence. Dak is brave and hates inaction, and in some ways is the opposite of his once-teacher Father Dain. Dak has been a monk since he was ten years old and does not remember much from before he became a Brother of the Dynasty.

Brother Dai-No-Kai: A middle-aged monk originally from Dusk Hill who feels he has been trapped in the mountainous southern temples for too much of his life. Willing for an adventure, Kai is brave but not foolhardy and has experience with combat - when he was as a young man, he was a soldier of Rosewick, but was gravely wounded in battle while serving Duke Henry, James II and Duke Gallance, thus being dismissed from the army.

Father Dain: One of the head Monks of the Dynasty, Father Dain's wisdom is incredible - but he is easily scared by the dark possibilities revealed by the orb that lie in wait ahead of all. Dain is otherwise kind, giving and extremely religious to the almighty Lord of the Afterlife.

GNOMES:

Baledor: The Gnomish son of Durbain, Baledor is a competent smith and fighter. He is relatively young for a Gnome, being only of fifty years.

Baledor feels constantly dwarfed by all those around him, and has yet to learn the art of friendship.

Buergat: Buergat is another Gnomish smith who is a friend of Durbain's.

Terrgon: Terrgon is another Gnomish smith who is a friend of Durbain's.

Durbain: Perhaps the greatest Gnomish smith in all the land. Living below the southern mountains where the temples of the Dynasty are, Durbain is comfortable in his home and in progress on a great undertaking: crafting his masterpiece.

ABOUT THE AUTHOR

Raphael White is twelve years old. He lives in the UK with his family and noisy dog. He has been writing fiction since the age of six and this is his first novella. Dungeons and Dragons are a big part of his life and one of his favourite activities is being a Dungeon Master, where he is known for embellishing storylines and escapades with poetry written in the moment. He is passionate about being a vegan and is a foodie, enjoying cooking and being creative with recipes. His other interests include coding, Minecraft and reading (of course).

Printed in Great Britain
by Amazon

72944911R00098